If For Any Reason
"Warm and inviting, *If For Any Reason* is a delightful read. I fell in love with these characters and with my time in Nantucket. Don't miss this one!"
Robin Lee Hatcher, Award-winning author of *Who I Am With You*

"*If For Any Reason* took me and my romance-loving heart on a poignant journey of hurt, hope, and second chances . . . From tender moments to family drama to plenty of sparks, this is a story to be savored. Plus, that Nantucket setting—I need to plan a trip pronto!"
Melissa Tagg, Award-winning author of *Now and Then and Always*

Just Let Go
"Walsh's charming narrative is an enjoyable blend of slice-of-life and small-town Americana that will please Christian readers looking for a sweet story of forgiveness."
Publishers Weekly

"Original, romantic, and emotional. Walsh doesn't just write the typical romance novel. . . . She makes you feel for all the characters, sometimes laughing and sometimes crying along with them."
Romantic Times

If For Any Reason *(a Nantucket Romance)*
Is it Any Wonder *(a Nantucket Romance)* April, 2021

HARBOR POINTE
Just Look Up
Just Let Go
Just One Kiss
Just Like Home

LOVES PARK, COLORADO
Paper Hearts
Change of Heart

SWEETHAVEN
A Sweethaven Summer
A Sweethaven Homecoming
A Sweethaven Christmas
A Sweethaven Romance (a novella)

Things Left Unsaid
Hometown Girl

A
Match Made
at Christmas

a Nantucket love story

Courtney Walsh

For my readers.
I am utterly humbled and grateful for you.

Visit Courtney Walsh's website at www.courtneywalshwrites.com.

A Match Made at Christmas

Cover designed by Jennifer MacKey of Seedlings Design

Edited by Charlene Patterson

The author is represented by Natasha Kern of Natasha Kern Literary, Inc.

PO Box 1069, White Salmon, WA 98672

For information about special discounts for bulk purchases, please contact Sweethaven Press at courtney@courtneywalsh.com

Library of Congress Cataloging-in-Publication Data

Printed in the United States of America

CHAPTER 1

DEFINITELY NOT A KISS

*I*t wasn't a real kiss.

That's what Prudence Sutton told herself as her best friend, Hayes McGuire, pulled away and studied her.

It wasn't a real kiss.

It was a *hello after months of not seeing each other* kiss. Never mind that it landed dangerously close to her lips. Or that the smell of his aftershave lingered in the air. Or that she'd considered turning toward him at the last moment just for the chance to taste the lips of this beautiful man.

Pull it together, Pru.

"I can't believe you're here." She smiled as he squeezed both of her arms, looking at her with that trademark lopsided grin, the one that had been melting women all across the globe since he first took his job as a travel writer. She fancied herself immune to it, and played the part of an eye-rolling, straight-talking best friend with an authentic flair no one could question.

But she'd been preparing for this face-to-face with Hayes for two weeks—ever since the day he texted to let her know he was coming.

"Are you kidding?" He smiled at her now. Had he had his teeth whitened? They practically gleamed. "I wasn't going to miss seeing your work honored." He slung a slouchy leather duffel over his shoulder and pushed a hand through the light brown hair that swooped sideways over his right eyebrow. He looked every bit the part of a world traveler, and that fact did nothing to calm her racing pulse.

"It's not that big of a deal." Prudence pulled her winter coat tighter around her, thankful she'd added the scarf—it was colder than she realized.

He waved her off, then draped his free arm over her shoulder and started walking away from the ferry dock.

"Nonsense," he said. "It's *such* a big deal the entire McGuire clan is coming in for the Festival of Trees."

"Hayes." She stopped. "You can't be serious."

He waggled his brows, and his hazel eyes sparkled with amusement. Her best friend façade was quickly crumbling.

"You know how they are," he said. "They heard about the tree, and they couldn't be stopped." He nudged her. "I don't think you understand what an honor this is, Pru."

She groaned. "Not enough of an honor that the entire family has to up and change their holiday plans to be here."

She felt, rather than saw, his shrug as they were now back to walking away from the ferry that had brought him to Nantucket after months and months away.

Finally, Hayes was home. And all it took was a Christmas tree.

And yeah, she supposed it was a little bit of a big deal. After all, the Festival of Trees was a big deal, and she'd been chosen to decorate the 20-foot tree at the top of Main Street. A tree with magical Christmas powers—it talked.

Everyone knew the secret of the illusion—a man with a microphone hiding up in the window of City Hall, right behind the tree. But nobody talked about that. It would spoil the magic. And around here, magic was precious.

Pru had never fancied herself an artist, but she had to admit, she was pretty jazzed having her work recognized by the town she'd adopted as her home.

"I'm not sure what I've come up with is going to go over very well," she said. "Surfing and Christmas don't exactly go together."

A small dinghy carrying a tiny, decorated Christmas tree bobbed in the harbor. A light dusting of snow blanketed Nantucket's cobblestone streets, which in a few days would be lined and lit with decorated Christmas trees.

Nantucket customarily was not known as a Christmas destination, but to Prudence, there was no better time to be on the island. The festivities kicked off the day after Thanksgiving with the tree lighting, and then a week later, the Christmas Stroll and the Festival of Trees. Because Pru was the artist who designed the talking tree this year, she would also have to attend a preview party a week from today, and she was thankful Hayes had agreed to be her plus-one. Attending fancy events alone had always made her feel like a loser.

As the owner of a small surf shop, her custom-made surfboards had garnered national attention last year when not one, but two pro surfers commissioned their own unique designs from Sutton Surf. An accomplished surfer in her own right, Pru had a great love for the Nantucket summer—but this time of year, when the island went still, that's when the world turned to magic.

"Want me to take a look?" Hayes asked as they reached her SUV. "Give me a private unveiling?"

"Why does it sound inappropriate when you say it?" She grinned at him, ignoring the patter of her heartbeat, considerably quicker than was probably healthy.

He smiled back. "I assure you I have nothing but honorable intentions toward you, m'lady."

Drat.

She got in the car and turned on the engine, rubbing her hands together and wondering if that would take the chill away.

"Thanks for picking me up," he said. "My family gets in tomorrow morning, so I had no way to get their island car down here."

She glanced over at him, still in a bit of shock he'd actually returned. Hayes didn't typically get the chance to come to Nantucket often, and almost never off-season. Hayes had visited the island for a few weeks the previous summer, but she'd been traveling, so it had been months since she'd seen him face-to-face.

The fact that he'd been so insistent on coming for the Christmas Stroll had both surprised and worried her.

"You're okay, right?" she asked.

He frowned. "'Course."

"I was surprised you wanted to come to the island for the holidays—that's not typical for you."

"Well, it's not typical for my best friend to be the artist selected to design the talking tree."

She studied him. What wasn't he telling her?

"Why are you looking at me like that?"

"Like what?" She put the car in reverse and slowly backed out of the parking lot and onto the street.

"Like you think there's more to the story." He shifted in the seat.

"Is there more to the story?" She steadied her gaze on the road in front of her as the sun faded and the moonlight began to shine.

"Nah," he said. "This trip is all about you, as it should be."

She liked the way that sounded. If she dwelled on it for too long, she might actually believe that his being here, like that hello kiss, was about a whole lot more than being a good friend.

But no, she'd set the tone for this relationship the day she and Hayes met ten years prior. She thought of that day often. Would things be different if she hadn't responded the way she did?

Hayes was a typical, cocky rich kid who thought too highly of himself. At least that's what she thought at the time. His group of guys came stocked with an entourage of bikini-clad, toned, blond girls, and Pru knew the type all too well.

So when he caught the same wave she did, the only thing she could think was *I'll show you how it's done, pretty boy.*

And she did. He wiped out almost instantly, but Pru

rode the wave all the way in with such precision, such finesse, it garnered the attention of not only Hayes, but his entire posse.

He'd met her on the beach as she packed her things, and that's when she first came face-to-face with his million-watt smile, the kind of smile that oozed charm and magnetism.

The wave hadn't taken her down, but that smile certainly could've.

"All right, that was impressive," he'd said.

"What was?"

He stuck the end of his board in the sand and grinned at her. "You kicking my butt out there," he said.

She smiled. "Oh, you noticed that, did you?"

"Let me take you to dinner," he said with such confidence it nearly knocked her sideways.

"Wow," she said. "That was bold."

His hair dripped onto his shoulder, and the droplets slid down his muscular torso.

He didn't break eye contact with her for a second. "What can I say? When I see something I like, I go for it."

She peered past him to the harem of blondes. "I bet you do."

He followed her gaze, then snapped his attention back to her. "I don't even know those girls."

She picked up her board and started off.

"At least tell me your name," he said.

She didn't respond.

"I'm going to find out," he said. "Might as well tell me."

She turned but kept walking backward. "What's the point? I'm not interested."

"Boyfriend?" He watched her—a little too intently.

"You think the only reason I might not be interested in you is because I'm taken?"

He shrugged, and the way the sunlight hit him, his bronze skin practically glowed.

One of the bikini girls bounced over and stood next to him, giving Pru a once-over. Prudence raised a brow, as if this was the perfect visual of an alternate reason she might not want to go out with him.

The blonde shimmied up next to his wet body, and Pru gave a mock salute. "See ya later, boss." She turned to go, but not before she caught the look on his face, one that seemed to have something to say but thought better of it.

And from that day on, she'd carefully kept him in the friend zone.

Things would be completely different if she'd responded to his advances that day.

Who was she kidding? There would be nothing between them if she'd responded differently that day. They might've had one or two amazing dates, but Hayes would've ended things the same way he did with every girl he dated. He seemed to find it impossible to get serious about any of them. She'd always said he'd left a trail of broken hearts all over the world.

At least hers wasn't one of them.

And at least now she could claim him as a friend. A good friend, in fact. The kind of friend who kissed her hello and made her feel like she wasn't alone. The kind of friend with a family who changed their holiday plans to support something as silly as her artwork.

Not that custom surfboards were a traditional canvas.

Regardless, she needed that. It wasn't like she had a family of her own.

She drew in a deep breath now, not at all aware of his woodsy scent that had filled the SUV.

"So, we'll do Thanksgiving dinner with my family, then the tree lighting and caroling downtown the day after. Then, didn't you say there's a party or something to kick off the Stroll and crown you the queen of the Festival of Trees this year?"

She groaned. "You do not have to do all of that. And I'm not the queen of anything. I'm just the artist who designed the 20-foot talking tree."

"Oh, is that all?" She didn't miss the sarcasm in his voice.

She could feel his eyes on her. She gripped the steering wheel and tried not to wonder how she looked from the side.

"Did you not hear me when I said this week is all about you? Don't pretend this isn't a big deal."

She braked at a stop sign and glanced over at him, which, it turned out, was a surefire way to lose her breath. His eyes looked older now, but they still glowed, and while he didn't talk about it, she suspected he'd suffered heartbreak too, though maybe not when it came to women. He wasn't serious enough about any of them to ever let himself get hurt.

Still, there were a lot of ways for a heart to break, and despite his image, she knew there was a depth to him that he hardly ever showed to anyone. And where there was depth, there was pain—and he'd seen too much in his travels to be exempt.

They were like two shattered pieces of glass, and she had to wonder if their pieces would ever fit together.

"Well, thank you for that," she said. "It means a lot to me."

He squeezed her hand, that familiar, mischievous smile playing at the corners of his lips. "You know I'd do anything for you, Pru."

A friendly honk from behind kept her from lingering there, and she stepped on the gas, begging herself to stay as calm and cool as she needed to be if she was going to keep up this charade.

And she must. Because if she lost Hayes, she would be hopelessly, horribly, utterly alone.

And that wasn't something she was willing to risk.

CHAPTER 2

The McGuire family had its own set of Thanksgiving traditions, so when Hayes mentioned he was flying to Nantucket to spend the holiday with Pru, he didn't expect his parents to come along.

Now, drawn from bed by the smell of freshly pressed coffee, he felt a smidge grateful they were that kind of family—the kind that would upend everything to support someone they considered "one of their own." And that was exactly how they saw Pru.

Hayes had been bringing her around for years now, and while he often got teased about it, he thought his family had mostly accepted the fact that the two of them were just friends.

After all, Pru was the exact opposite of the girls he usually dated. He'd met his last girlfriend, Delilah, around the same time he'd met Prudence. He and Delilah reconnected a little over a year ago at a party in Manhattan. Hayes had just returned from Taiwan, and Delilah had just shot her first magazine cover. The leggy blond model asked him out, and they dated for a few months before Hayes called it quits.

"Why don't you ever date intelligent women, Hayes? You're one of the smartest people I know," Pru had said when she found out he and Delilah were together. He'd spent more time with Delilah than he typically spent with any of the women he dated, but still, he knew better than to get serious about her.

That had happened once—a girl in college named Kara. Kara *had* been smart. And funny. And beautiful. And also still hung up on a high school boyfriend who eventually wormed his way back into her heart. And her bed.

Hayes had fallen hard and fast for Kara, and when he discovered her betrayal, he'd made up his mind to never let that happen again. Now, he dated casually, made friends easily, and never let his heart get tied up in the mix. When he needed a date for a media event, he had a handful of beautiful women he could call, but they all knew Hayes wasn't a relationship guy.

He kept things simple, and he was always clear up front. Things were better this way—and he could avoid ever feeling the sting of betrayal again.

Not that he'd ever explained that to Pru. Though he'd downplayed the whole situation with Kara, Hayes was pretty sure Pru knew he'd had his heart broken. He wasn't sure what she believed about him these days, but probably that he was a never-too-serious, fun-loving guy who dated too many women and had no interest in settling down.

She'd be right about very little of that—but why ruin the image?

The less she really knew about his feelings, the better. Especially his feelings about her, given the fact that every time they were together, he was unsure of them.

She had this way of looking at him that made him feel completely naked—and not in a good way. He knew that as much as he tried to, there was no hiding from Prudence Sutton. Which meant his tried-and-true *keep everyone at an arm's length* approach to life was lost on her.

That comforted and terrified him at the same time.

The McGuire family had been spending summers in Nantucket for as long as Hayes could remember, though he didn't get back nearly as often as he would've liked, and when he did, his stays were short. He missed it. It was calming; like if he let himself, he could imagine being ten-years-old and spending long, lazy days out in the sun, hunting for seashells or building sandcastles right there on the beach behind the family cottage.

His family didn't come from money, but his father had learned about smart investing, and thankfully, he'd passed down what he knew to his kids. And Hayes had reaped the benefits. He was proud of his portfolio these days.

In all his life, Hayes could only remember spending Thanksgiving on the island two other times, and frankly, he was happy to have a reason to be here. The second he'd stepped off the ferry, something inside him settled, as if that wanderlust that usually drove him forward finally found a reason to park and turn off its engine.

He stared at the ceiling, listening to the sound of distant voices below. The room still looked like it belonged to a kid, with its navy blue, white, and red nautical theme. Hayes didn't even mind, though he could do with a few more inches at the end of the full-sized bed.

He stumbled downstairs and found the house full, as expected. His family was set to arrive on the first ferry that morning, and he figured they'd have Thanksgiving dinner in the works as soon as they walked through the door. How had he slept through their arrival?

Hollis, and his fiancée, Emily, sat on the couch, and at their feet, a lolling Tilly, Hollis's black lab.

"Morning, brother." Hollis stood, clapped a hand on Hayes's shoulder, then gave him a shove.

Emily stood and gave him a hug.

"All right, that's good," Hollis said, a tease in his voice. He pulled Emily from Hayes's embrace. "Don't want you moving in on my girl."

Emily rolled her eyes.

Hayes moved into the kitchen and poured himself a cup of coffee. His mother kissed his cheek and his father gave him a nod over the financial section of the newspaper.

"When does Pru get here?" his mom asked.

He leaned against the counter. "You said three for dinner, right?"

Mom scoffed. "She could've come earlier—we'd love to spend as much time with her as possible. We missed her this summer. And we want to celebrate with her."

Pru had spent most of this past summer traveling, while employees ran the surf shop. Her absence had been noticed the few weeks he'd been on the island between assignments. Her boards had gotten national attention, and she'd spent the summer attending the pro competitions while he watched on TV for a glimpse of her.

Once, he'd spotted Jackson Dupree, a hard-bodied surfing phenom from Hawaii, with his arm draped around Prudence in a familiar way that suggested the two of them were a little more than friendly. Jackson stuck his tongue out for the camera, sporting the "hang loose" sign with his hand and then turned and kissed Pru, fully on the mouth. When the surfer pulled away, the stunned look on Pru's face matched the way Hayes felt. Shocked and a little nauseous.

"This girl is the real deal," Jackson said with a grin.

Hayes had turned the TV off, then thrown the remote, bothered, but unsure why. Pru had dated over the years, of course she had—she was the best of everything—but what he'd just seen felt like disrespect, and he wished he could be there to protect her.

Never mind that Prudence Sutton had been sticking up for herself since long before the day he met her.

"This is quite an honor," his father said from behind the paper. "Being chosen to create the talking tree."

Hayes pushed a hand through his messy hair. "Yeah, it is. It's about time people started noticing how amazing she is."

He didn't miss the knowing look that pinballed around the room.

"What?" Hayes set his mug on the counter.

Mom heaved a bag of potatoes onto the counter. "Nothing, dear."

"We just agree is all," his father said. "It's about time *people* started noticing how amazing she is."

Hayes tossed his dad a quizzical look and glanced at Hollis for some help. His brother's blank expression told him to keep looking.

"Look, just don't make her feel weird," Hayes said. "She

already thinks you guys are crazy for coming to the island at all."

Mom frowned. "She does?"

"Mom, you changed your entire holiday plan," Hayes said. "I mean, how long has it been since you've done Thanksgiving on the island?"

"All the more reason to do it," she said. "I had forgotten how beautiful it is here this time of year. Besides, we changed our plans for Prudence. Isn't she worth it?"

"'Course she is," he said. "But she doesn't know that."

Mom eyed him. "I gather there's a lot Pru doesn't know."

He frowned. "What's that supposed to mean?"

The door opened and Harper, the youngest McGuire sibling and only sister, stumbled in. "I forgot how cold it is here."

And just like that, the attention shifted from Hayes to Harper. He breathed a sigh of relief and made a note to thank his sister later for her impeccable timing.

Now, to survive an entire holiday dinner with Prudence sitting beside him and this nosy family who didn't seem as settled on their relationship status as he'd thought.

As a travel writer, Hayes had seen the world. He'd done some serious hustling for more than a decade, and a few years ago, he realized he could slow down a smidge and reap the fruits of his labor. He'd been smart about building his brand. He'd written books and magazine articles on high end travel on a shoestring budget, and with the money he earned from sponsors of his blog and YouTube channel, he'd built up a tiny empire. Multiple revenue streams plus smart investing afforded Hayes the luxury of a few weeks off.

And it couldn't have come at a better time. After months of roaming, he needed a place to land. The cottage had always felt like home, much more so than his nearly empty apartment in Boston.

Hayes had eaten dinner in so many different cultures, he'd lost count. But nothing—nothing—compared to being with his family on a holiday. In all his time away, he'd made it a point to come home for Thanksgiving and Christmas whenever he could, and he could count on one hand how many times he'd missed a holiday meal.

It didn't matter where they were, Nan McGuire knew how to make a meal special. Today was no different.

The guest list was relatively small—Mom said she wanted time to talk with every person there, and if there were too many, there wouldn't be time enough—so it was the immediate family plus Prudence, Emily, and Hayes's Aunt Nellie and Uncle Arthur.

Nellie and Hayes's dad, Jeffrey, were siblings, and they still bickered like kids. It made for entertaining dinner conversation.

Pru fit in with the rest of them like she was what she was—one of the family. Harper had told him once if he ever did get serious about someone, he would have a strange situation on his hands because Pru wasn't going anywhere—they wouldn't allow it. Whoever he brought into the fold at this point was going to feel competitive with her whether it was warranted or not.

He'd mostly ignored his sister, and wasn't sure why he

was thinking about it now. He was so far from a serious relationship these days it wasn't even worth considering.

"So, how about you, Hayes?" Aunt Nellie asked him now, moments after they'd all taken their seats around a table decorated so perfectly it should've been photographed and submitted to a magazine.

Brown paper had been laid over a cream-colored tablecloth, and instead of place cards, his mom had used white paint to hand-letter each of their names right at each place setting. In the middle of the table were sprigs of greenery in small vases, tealight candles staggered in between. Cloth napkins were neatly folded on each plate, stacked with silverware. The best part about it was that none of the pieces matched. No two plates or forks or glasses were the same. Even the napkins were unique, and yet somehow, his mother put it all together perfectly.

Hayes painted on his trademark smile and met his aunt's gaze from across the table. "How about me, Aunt Nellie?" He liked verbally sparring with her and found her almost as worthy an opponent as Pru.

"How long are you planning on staying on the island?" Aunt Nellie asked as she piled a scoop of mashed potatoes onto her plate. "Knowing you, I expect you'll be running around the world again by this time next week."

Hayes couldn't even consider another trip right now. He'd been away too long, and he needed time to recover from more than just jet lag.

"Not true, Aunt Nellie." Prudence set her water glass on the table. "He's agreed to accompany me to the Festival of Trees Preview Party next Thursday."

"Is that right? So you'll be around for a bit?" Aunt Nellie eyed him from behind her bifocals. The woman wasn't old—maybe early sixties—but those glasses said otherwise. Everything else about her was spry and full of life.

"I haven't decided yet." He glanced at Pru. "I'm not in a hurry to get back to work."

Hollis set his glass down and looked at Hayes. "That's not like you."

Hayes shrugged. "I'm due for a break. It's okay that I stick around for a little while, right, Ma?"

"Of course, Hayes," his mother said. "As long as you promise to stop calling me 'Ma.'"

Hayes flashed her a smile, then found Aunt Nellie watching him. She seemed to be reading into his choice to stick around. She did that—read between the lines. She picked up on the things you didn't say and said them for you.

Aunt Nellie was his favorite aunt. She'd visited his family one summer on Nantucket ages ago and liked it so much she moved here year-round. She met and married Arthur, a local, and that sealed the deal. She now said she had no use for the mainland at all.

It was the strangest thing because Nellie didn't grow up on the island or come from money, and yet somehow, the woman fit in with every social class a person would find on Nantucket.

She could shoot the breeze with the lobstermen as easily as she could take tea with the rich ladies who bought only designer clothes, purses, and shoes. Aunt Nellie was a chameleon that way.

"That's kind of you," Nellie said now. "To take time out to spend the holidays here."

"Yeah, despite what you've heard, I'm actually a nice guy."

At his side, Pru shifted.

"And you know how much I love a good party," he said quickly, hoping the conversation hadn't made her feel like a charity case.

"Oh, we know," they all seemed to say in unison.

He'd have to play the part a little while longer—Hayes, the one who was never serious. Hayes, the flirt. Hayes, the party boy. Because if he didn't, his family might catch on that he'd changed. And he wasn't ready to discuss the reasons why.

They ate. They laughed. They watched football. They went for a walk on the beach. They ate leftovers. They drank wine. They told jokes. They played Scrabble. And when it got to be 10:00 p.m., a quiet (or maybe a fullness?) came over everyone, seemingly at the same time. They were scattered throughout the lower level of the cottage, Hayes and Pru sat on the couch, a fire flickering in the fireplace beside them.

He imagined from the outside, the cottage probably looked a bit idyllic, and maybe it was. Maybe some places were still safe.

"Well, that's it for me." Aunt Nellie stood. Arthur, who hardly ever spoke, followed suit, then retrieved his wife's things from Hayes's parents' first-floor bedroom. He returned, wearing his coat and holding hers, then stood off to the side, clutching her purse like a nineteenth-century butler.

"Hayes."

Hayes glanced up and found he had Nellie's full attention. She narrowed her gaze, zeroing in on him, then beckoned him closer with the wag of her finger.

He rose from his place on the sofa and followed her over to where Arthur stood like a statue.

As she pulled her coat on, she looked up at Hayes. "Come visit me tomorrow. There's something I need to talk to you about."

Hayes frowned. What on earth could Aunt Nellie have to discuss with him?

"Is it about traveling because I can—"

"Oh no," she said. "Well, sort of. Just show up around lunchtime, okay?" She squeezed his arm.

"Okay, Aunt Nellie."

"Very good." Another squeeze. "Oh, and Hayes, you darling boy, when are you going to find a nice girl and settle down?"

His throat went dry.

"Your father says you have no trouble finding dates, but your relationships have a way of ending before they really begin."

"Aunt Nellie, I'm not sure why—"

She flicked her hand in the air. "All I'm saying is, you don't want to wait too long." She tossed a glance to the sofa where Pru sat, a strange look on her face. "If you do, all the good ones will be taken."

"Thanks, Aunt Nellie." He ushered her to the door.

"I'll see you tomorrow."

He let her and his uncle out into the wild and turned to face his family, who all took that as an opportunity to chatter on and on about Hayes's love life.

Prudence, he noticed, didn't say a word.

CHAPTER 3

MATCHMAKING AND MAGIC

*W*hen Aunt Nellie moved to Nantucket, she rented a room from an older woman whose name Hayes couldn't remember.

After she met Arthur, they bought a sprawling cottage right on the ocean. Arthur had money—a lot of it—so now Nellie did too. He'd never understood their relationship, but who was he to judge? He obviously wasn't an authority.

Nellie and Arthur had two children, both of whom visited the island every third year or so. And while Nellie would never say it, Hayes suspected she'd always favored him over her own two kids.

He stood on the steps of that sprawling cottage, which had been well maintained all these years, and waited for her to open the door. The cottage was decked out for Christmas already, white lights along the edge of the roof and a giant, white-lit wreath on the front door. Aunt Nellie was a pistol, but she knew how to make things look good.

The door opened and she gave him a wry smile. Her dyed red hair fell in waves to her shoulders, and she wore a flowy pair of pants that swished as she turned and walked away, motioning for him to follow.

He did—straight into her study, a spacious room with a fireplace, two sofas, a desk, and a whole wall of built-in bookshelves piled high with books he was certain Nellie had never read.

"What's up?" he asked, wanting to put an end to his confusion.

She sat down on one sofa, then motioned for him to sit across from her on the other one. "Let's chat."

Hayes sat down, leaned back into the couch, and did his best to look unruffled. Nellie had a way of putting people on the spot. He vowed to be ready for her.

"I'm sure you're wondering why I asked you here," she said.

"Especially since you haven't offered me anything to eat."

As if on cue, Marta, Nellie's live-in housekeeper, appeared in the doorway. "Lunch is ready in the dining room, ma'am."

Nellie didn't look away but held Hayes's gaze with a knowing smile.

"Well, what do you know?" he said, amused.

"Shall we?" She stood and sashayed in her swishy pants out of the room and into the dining room, which had a lovely view of the ocean.

"Seems we could've come out here in the first place, skipped the study altogether, but who am I to criticize?" Hayes sat down at the neatly set table, facing the water.

"Marta wasn't ready," Nellie said.

He nodded. "And it's important that you impress me why?"

She laughed. "Well, it is, in fact, important to impress you because I'm about to ask you for a huge favor."

He glanced down at his plate. A large turkey club on toasted homemade bread and a pile of homemade potato chips stole his attention for a split second. A fresh dill pickle topped off the meal and only then did Hayes realize how hungry he was.

"Can I dig in?" he asked. "While you pitch whatever crazy idea you have now."

"Yes, eat." Then she rolled her eyes. "Why would you think I have a crazy idea?"

"Aunt Nellie, it's what you're known for." He took a bite of his sandwich, got a zesty hint of ranch, and decided to eat slowly to savor it. "Tell Marta this is amazing."

"Tell her yourself." Nellie smirked as she positioned a white cloth napkin on her lap, then took a sip of her iced tea. "But first, tell me why you're really in Nantucket."

He chewed, then swallowed, enjoying the bite as any man in his right mind would. "I told you why. I came for Pru."

"Well." Nellie set her drink down. "I didn't think you'd be so forthcoming with that little tidbit."

He rolled his eyes. "Don't start. Pru is my friend. She's practically one of the guys."

"Not with that figure she's not." Nellie laughed.

Hayes nearly choked on a potato chip. "Aunt Nellie."

She held up a hand in surrender. "Sorry. I meant it as a compliment. That girl is very well-built. Puts the rest of them to shame."

23

"The rest of who?"

"The frivolous ones," she said, as if he shouldn't have had to ask. "The girls you usually spend time with."

"I don't date as much as you seem to think I do," he said.

"Oh, I know," Nellie said. "I just don't understand why you're wasting time with relationships that don't really matter to you when you have someone like Prudence in your life."

Hayes took a drink. "We're friends, Aunt Nellie."

"I know, I know," she said. "But an aunt can dream. I like Prudence. Reminds me of myself a whole lot of years ago. I'm glad you have a friend like her."

He eyed her for a moment, trying to find the catch, then cautiously said, "Thank you."

"And I do think it's wonderful they selected her to be the artist to design the talking tree this year."

"It is, right?" Hayes took another bite. "She's downplaying it, but it's a huge deal. And if anyone deserves to be recognized, it's Pru. She works her fingers to the bone most days, even in the off season."

Nellie nodded. Then she got quiet, and he suspected she was about to tell him whatever it was she'd asked him to come for.

He wiped his hands on his napkin and looked at her. "You're not dying, are you?"

Nellie laughed. "Heavens, no. Why would you think so?"

"You're being strange." He eyed her. "I mean, stranger than normal."

A flash of amusement flittered across her face. "The

truth is, I'm still making up my mind about whether or not I should ask you this favor."

"Aunt Nellie, what is it?"

She pushed her plate away and folded her hands on the table. "Your Uncle Arthur has given me such a good life."

"Is he dying?"

"Hayes," she said, "nobody is dying."

"Well, that's a relief," he said. "Next time you decide to be weird, maybe lead with that."

"Can I finish?" She flashed him a wry smile.

He motioned with his hand for her to continue—as if he could stop her.

"Arthur doesn't ever ask me for anything," she said. "He does whatever I want, gives me everything I want, lives the life in the house that I wanted on the island that I love."

"Well, he's crazy about you," Hayes said, though he wasn't sure why. After all, Arthur showed about as much emotion as a dryer sheet. But even so, it was obvious how much he loved Nellie. Hayes was surprised to realize it, but he was kind of jealous of their relationship.

"Anyway," she continued, "after all this time, he finally asked me to do something, and I simply can't say no."

"Okay," Hayes said, still confused at what she was getting at.

"Christmas in Paris," she said.

Slowly, he dropped his hands to the table and nodded. "So, you do need my travel advice."

"No," she said. "I've got the trip planned right down to the hour. We are going to have the most marvelous time, my dear, don't you doubt that for a second."

"I don't," he said. "Paris at Christmas is magical."

"Magical." She smiled. "Hayes, I need to show you something."

He frowned. "Okay."

"But I need your word that this will stay between us."

"Now you're freaking me out." Although that word *now* was misleading. He'd been on the edge of freaking out since she'd asked him to come over the night before.

She stood. "Follow me." She started off in the direction of the stairs. "Do you know anything about Noni Rose?"

"Uh, yeah. She's a Nantucket legend," Hayes said, trying to remember. "A famous matchmaker. Some say she works in secret, behind the scenes, even now."

"She does." Nellie started up the stairs. "She has been for years."

"You think she's real?"

Nellie stopped and looked at him. "I know she's real."

Hayes paused on the steps and looked up at her, noting a strange twinkle in her eye.

"Years ago, I came to Nantucket seeking a new life. I was visiting your parents when I met a woman named Helen who took a shine to me right away."

Helen. Right.

They were at the top of the stairs now, and Hayes realized he hadn't been up here since he was a kid. "What does that mean, 'took a shine' to you? Like, she had a crush on you?"

"Hayes Michael McGuire." Nellie swatted him across the arm.

"I'm just trying to make sense of what you're saying."

"Helen saw something in me." She led him to the room at the end of the long hallway. "She said I had a gift. Said I could read people, that I knew what they needed even when they didn't. She said the magic had found me."

Hayes searched her eyes for any clue that would explain what she was trying to say. He didn't want to roll his eyes, but he wondered if she'd finally lost her mind.

"Said she wanted to train me to be her replacement."

As far as he knew, Nellie had never worked a day in her life, so he was even more confused now, trying to figure out what this Helen could've possibly wanted from his aunt.

"I lived in her house for several months, and then she introduced me to Arthur. She said we were soulmates." Nellie put her hand on the doorknob of a room at the end of the hall but didn't open it. "She was right. Helen was always right when it came to love."

"That's great, Aunt Nellie," Hayes said. "Sounds like a great lady."

Nellie pushed the door open, revealing a small room with light pink walls. At the center was a desk, piled high with file folders, and on the wall were two large bulletin boards full of photos, newspaper articles, thank-you cards, and a bunch of paraphernalia he couldn't decipher upon first glance.

"Is this your office?"

"Of sorts," she said, an air of mystery coming over her. "This is the office of Noni Rose."

Hayes turned and looked at her, confusion—he was sure—on his face. He shook his head, trying to understand what she was saying.

"*I* am Noni Rose," she said, filling in the blanks.

"Aunt Nellie, that's not possible," he said.

"Sit." She motioned to the chair on one side of the desk,

then took her seat behind it. "Helen explained that she'd been plucked out of obscurity by a woman who'd been working as Noni Rose. That woman had also been chosen by the Noni Rose before her and on and on as far back as the history of Nantucket. As long as people have been on this island, the famous matchmaker has been at work."

"So, you're saying it's a lie that's passed down from generation to generation?" Hayes took his seat, crossed his ankle over his knee, and waited for an answer.

"Oh dear," she said. "Maybe this was a mistake."

"What was, telling me that one of the island's oldest legends is a bunch of hogwash?" He laughed. "Pretty sure I already knew that. I don't believe in soulmates or magic or any of that."

"I see," she said. "You're a doubter."

"A doubter?"

"A doubting Thomas, like the man in the Bible—"

"Yeah, I know who Thomas was," Hayes said. "You're equating me not believing in matchmakers with Thomas not believing in Jesus?"

She laughed. "Look, all I'm saying is, I've had a pretty successful run. Helen found me when I was very young, and this is all part of the reason I stayed on the island."

He wasn't sure what to make of her story, but he surely didn't believe love worked this way, so mostly he wanted to tell her this was ludicrous.

"Do you need proof of my success?" she asked, and he could tell by her tone that she had it.

"Sure," he said. "Let's see what you've got."

She pulled a small book out of the desk and handed it to him. He opened it and found the names of several couples written on the pages throughout the book. In some cases, these names were accompanied by wedding announcements clipped from the newspaper and glued onto the page.

As he flipped, he began to see names and faces he recognized. "You're telling me *you're* the reason all of these people met and fell in love?"

She smiled smugly. "And I'll have you know of all my couples, only one has ever ended in a divorce."

He gave her a nod. Okay, that was impressive, if it was true. "Well done, Aunt Nellie. That's saying something these days."

"Helen explained that it was a very special kind of person who possessed the magic of being a matchmaker. She said it was important that the tradition was passed down so the romance of the island would live on."

"No offense, Aunt Nellie, but don't you think the romance of the island will go on whether you're matchmaking or not? Some might argue this is just you sticking your nose in other people's business."

She folded her hands and leaned in closer, across the desk. "Dear boy. Love might prevail here on the island, but it always benefits from the nudge of Noni Rose."

Hayes had no reply. His aunt might be certifiable, but he didn't feel like now was a good time to tell her so.

"And, furthermore, nobody knows anything about what I'm doing. I can assure you, there is nothing untoward happening here. I look at this as a responsibility, and I didn't ask for it, mind you. You don't get to choose to be Noni Rose, Noni Rose chooses you." She stared at him, an expectant look on her face.

He smiled at her. Had she just said something important and he misunderstood?

"I think it's a great thing, then," he said. "If it makes you happy, and people are finding love or whatever, more power to you."

"People do not find love *or whatever*," she said pointedly. "I create an atmosphere that allows love to blossom, that's all."

He didn't respond.

"And, you'll be pleased to know that I've selected my replacement."

"You're retiring from matchmaking?"

"I'm taking a little break."

"Right," he said. "Paris."

"Right." She nodded, that knowing expression still on her face.

"Aunt Nellie," he said. "What are you trying to say?"

"It's you, Hayes," she said with enthusiasm, as if he'd been chosen the next contestant on *The Price is Right*.

"What's me?"

"My replacement." She still leaned forward across the desk, but now it almost felt like she was luring him in somehow. "Well, temporarily."

"Me? No." He shook his head. "You've officially lost your mind."

"I know it seems crazy, kiddo, but Helen always told me when you know, you know." She eyed him. "And I know."

"Well, *I* know that you are crazy," he said. "Noni Rose is a *woman*."

She shrugged. "Doesn't have to be."

He stared at her, trying to determine exactly how

serious she was. Judging by her unchanging expression —very.

"Dudes do not become matchmakers," he said.

"It's a temporary gig," she repeated, as if that made it better.

"It's a gig I don't want," he said.

"Hayes, I didn't want to bring it up, but you do know that you were the only family member who didn't make it home for my birthday party in September."

September. Right. He should've come home for the party. In hindsight, that would've saved him a world of grief. "The only one?"

She nodded. "And, I might add, you *are* my favorite so I was especially disappointed."

He grinned. "I'm your favorite."

Aunt Nellie smiled back. "As if you didn't know." She pulled a photo out of her top desk drawer and slid it across the desk. "This is the woman I'm working on matching, and I just have a feeling if I leave for Paris without a replacement, it's not going to happen for her."

He looked at the photo. A plain-looking woman with kind eyes looked back at him. She was familiar. "Why her?"

"It's hard to explain. It's a feeling. It's like the Lord puts someone in my path, and I just know."

"So, nobody is asking you to do anything," he said.

"Technically, no," she said. "But it's a feeling. Something happens, and it's obvious this person needs my help. It's like a light bulb going off, or an idea popping into your head. Like magic."

"That's not magic, Aunt Nellie," he said. "That's nosi-

31

ness. And maybe a little blasphemous if you're trying to bring the Lord into it."

"You don't understand," she said. "But you will."

He shook his head. "I won't."

"It's just while I'm gone," she said. "Christmas is the most magical time for matchmaking. Do you know since I started, I've had a successful match every single Christmas? It's because magic makes the air electric. It's easy. And trust me, you will be great at this."

He shook his head. "Why on earth would you think this would be something I would want to do?"

She shrugged. "You're great with people. You know how to get them to open up. You're charming and everyone likes you. Plus, I think you have a sixth sense about these things."

"I don't."

She squinted, sizing him up. "Well, if I'm wrong, no harm done. But if I'm right, one Miss Peggy Swinton finds the love of her life."

"I can't do this, Aunt Nellie," he said. "I'm only here for a couple of weeks."

"You can and you will," she said. "And I think you're going to make a wonderful matchmaker. Trust me. I'm never wrong about these things."

"I would be a terrible matchmaker, Aunt Nellie," he said. "I don't even believe in love."

She scoffed. "Nonsense. You just need to see the magic for yourself."

Hayes tried not to roll his eyes. He had a feeling he wasn't going to be able to argue his way out of this one. Nellie obviously had her mind made up, and everyone knew when Nellie had her mind made up, there was no changing it.

"It's only until I return from Paris, and then I will let you retire." She waved him off. "You're the only one I've even considered for this job, Hayes, you should know that. I believe you have a gift."

He drew in a deep breath and let it out in one long stream. "You're not going to let me out of this, are you?"

She only smiled.

He groaned. "I know I'm gonna regret this."

But Aunt Nellie was unconcerned with his concerns and had already moved on to explaining the rules.

And that's how Hayes McGuire became Noni Rose, the famous Nantucket matchmaker.

CHAPTER 4

150 BALSAM TREES AND COBBLESTONE STREETS

*S*ometimes when Prudence got to working on a board, she completely lost track of time.

Other times, like when she was going to be meeting Hayes McGuire to go to the tree lighting, she watched the clock tick off the minutes with all the speed of a sleeping sloth.

Now, only fifteen minutes before he was scheduled to arrive, she stood in front of the mirror trying to decide if her outfit conveyed the appropriate amount of nonchalance.

She'd gone to the shop earlier that day, but she couldn't focus. She had two custom orders with deadlines, and they needed to get finished, but just knowing Hayes was back on the island had destroyed her sense of calm.

She'd gone to Thanksgiving dinner and, as she'd expected, he treated her just like one of his siblings. She might as well have been his blood relative for as much attention as he gave her. And she was fine with that. After all, she loved the McGuire family, and they clearly loved her.

Like a daughter.

She was practically one of them.

She should be grateful. Not every girl had another family on standby, ready and waiting with open arms. Pru's real parents lived in New Jersey. Or Ohio now. She couldn't remember. She'd come to Nantucket for a job one summer after high school and never left.

And they'd never come to visit.

Needless to say, it wasn't a great relationship.

But the McGuires had shown her that families could be wonderful. Every misconception she had about mothers and fathers and their kids had been disproven because of Hayes and his family. They got into each other's business. They teased each other. They were there for each other. They were friends. So, for them to practically adopt her was a gift.

And she should be grateful. Not sad that their middle son didn't view her as anything other than a good buddy.

Tonight, Prudence had curled her long dark hair, letting it fall in waves down her back. She wore a pair of dark jeans, a cream cowl neck sweater, and brown boots. Did the outfit say *I'm not trying to impress you?* She considered changing for the thirty-seventh time, but the knock on the door told her she was out of time.

She raced down from her bedroom, which overlooked the main living area of the small cottage. The house was tiny, but she'd worked hard to turn it into something she was proud of. The wood floors had been refinished and now had a natural, elegant feel to them. The walls were white shiplap, but she'd found a lot of ways to infuse the space with color. Pillows, rugs, artwork—all explosions of creativity—and, of course, there was a custom turquoise and pink surfboard hanging on the wall above the sofa.

She pulled the door open and found Hayes standing there, looking like he'd just swallowed a goldfish. "What's wrong with you?"

He stared at her.

"Are you sweating? It's freezing outside. Why are you sweating?" She pulled him by the arm, tugging him across the threshold and into her cottage.

He looked around. "It looks completely different in here."

"Yeah, well, it's been over a year and a half since you've been inside."

"And you're a famous surfboard artist now," he said.

She frowned. "Why do you look flushed? Are you sick?"

"Can I have some water?"

Only then did she realize he had a box tucked under his arm. "What's that?"

"Water, please."

She eyed him for a second, then motioned for him to sit down on the couch. She grabbed a bottle of water from the refrigerator and walked it back into the living room. One big, open floor plan made the cottage feel a lot more spacious. Never mind that her lofted bedroom was also in plain view.

The cottage suited her. And it was rare that she had company. Especially male company.

She sat down in the armchair across from him. "Do you want to skip the tree lighting? This really isn't that important."

"No," he said. He chugged half the bottle of water. "I just need a minute. And it is a big deal. They're lighting the tree you designed."

She glanced at the box. "You gonna tell me what's in there?"

He didn't look at her. "I don't think I'm supposed to."

She frowned. "Then why did you bring it?"

He found her eyes. "Because maybe I want you to accidentally open it?"

"Is there something dead inside there?"

"What? No." He stared at her for long enough to make her insides quake.

Which infuriated her because she knew better. She knew *this* man, of all men, was not going to ever—ever—look at her as anything other than a friend.

But he was her person. And she was grateful he was in her life, in whatever capacity she could have him. In the only capacity she could have him.

Her mind began to wander, probably because she was thinking the words "have him" after an already heightened awareness that he was practically in her bedroom, which inadvertently led her thoughts down a very long and winding road from which she wasn't sure she wanted to return.

"Pru."

His voice called her back to reality. She really needed to get a hold of herself. This crush was worse than she thought. She looked at him. His brow was knit in a straight line, and he looked genuinely concerned. Happy-go-lucky Hayes McGuire was . . . worried?

"Why do you seem so shaken up?" she asked.

"Open the box." His knee was bouncing—a surefire

indication that he was panicked.

Her imagination ran off, and before she could catch it, she'd decided he'd found proof of his adoption or a death certificate with his own name on it or maybe a map that led to a sunken ship full of gold.

Instead, what she found inside the box was a small scrapbook, a stack of papers, some photos, and a small notebook labeled "The Rules."

"What's this?"

"That is from my Aunt Nellie," he said. "Who has decided to pass down a very special tradition. To me."

She thumbed through the scrapbook. Photos and names of various couples looked back at her. "What tradition?"

He waited until she met his eyes, stopped bouncing his knee, and leveled his gaze on her. "The tradition of Noni Rose."

Pru frowned. "The matchmaker?"

"Yep."

"I don't understand."

Hayes took a breath, then unloaded the most unbelievable story she'd ever heard. Not nearly as dramatic as his being adopted or discovering a lost treasure would've been, but unbelievable because *What on earth was Aunt Nellie thinking?*

He stopped talking and looked at her.

"Did I say that out loud?"

He nodded.

"It just seems a bit crazy, doesn't it? I mean you—the notorious bachelor. You're not married. You're not even in a relationship. Have you ever even had a real relationship? Would you even know how?"

He eyed her. "It's nice to know you think so little of me."

There was something about the way he said it that made her wonder if she'd hurt his feelings. "I'm sorry."

"It's fine," he said. "And I don't completely disagree with you. It does seem a little crazy."

"Then why did you say you would do it?"

He sank into the couch and let his head rest on the wall behind him. He released a heavy sigh. "She guilted me into it."

Pru shook her head. "How?"

"She flattered me and told me she had a sense about me. Said I could read people. That I could disarm them. Said I was the only person she'd even considered asking to do this big favor for her."

"Ah, so she stroked your ego," Pru said.

"I guess."

She grabbed a pillow and tossed it at him, hitting him square in the face. "Then it serves you right. You let your pride get you here, Hayes McGuire."

He stuffed the pillow on his lap and leaned forward over the top of it. "This is crazy, Pru. I'm not a matchmaker."

She watched him. "So, don't do it."

He frowned. "I can't back out. I gave her my word."

It was odd to see him so conflicted over something that didn't really seem that important.

"When a McGuire gives his word, he means it," Hayes said.

"Your dad said that, right?"

He shrugged. "Who else?"

Hayes might be a commitment-phobe, but he was a

39

good person. His parents had seen to it that he was. And now, as he looked at her with those big hazel eyes, it nearly left her undone.

"Will you help me?"

"Me?" Prudence knew even less about relationships than Hayes did.

"Yes, you're the only person who knows." He reached for her hand and she forced herself not to think about how it felt to touch his skin. "The only person who can ever know."

She leaned forward and whispered, "Are you going to get struck by lightning for blabbing this to me?"

He leaned forward too, close enough that their faces were only a few inches apart. "I hope so," he whispered. "Then I won't have to become a matchmaker."

They sat like that for several seconds, both leaning toward the other one. In other circumstances, had they been different people, perhaps they may have ended the exchange kissing furiously on the couch.

But because they were who they were, they simply grinned at each other and pretended there was absolutely nothing electric in the air between them.

Well, she pretended. It was likely Hayes didn't feel that spark at all.

"Pru." He scooted over to the loveseat where she sat and faced her, practically on the same cushion as she was. "I'm not a matchmaker."

He was close to her now, like a friend, she told herself. But if she happened to fall just a few inches, their faces would end up dangerously close to each other again.

"You know I can't do this without you."

"Hayes, as terrible as your relationships have been,

mine have been worse," she said.

"Like you and that Hawaiian surfer?"

She straightened. "What Hawaiian surfer?"

"The one who kissed you on national television?"

He saw that?

"You made him a board, right?"

She looked away. "I set him straight real fast."

Hayes went still. "Did he hurt you?"

She looked at him. "No, of course not." Not really. Not the way he was thinking. Yes, he was too forward and yes, he might've touched her inappropriately, but Prudence Sutton was nobody's fool. She took care of him without a second thought. "But he's not allowed to ride on my boards anymore."

"Wow," he said. "Impressive."

She smiled. "I can handle myself."

"I know you can." He glanced at the box. "And you can handle this too."

She shook her head. "Are we leaving? Because if yes, we need to go. Main Street is probably already crawling with people."

He sighed as he stood. "Fine. But think about it, okay?"

"Fine." She pulled her coat on, fished her gloves out of the pockets, and found a stocking cap in a box by the front door.

"You gonna put that on?" he asked.

She glanced up. "I was going to. Keeps the head warm."

He smiled.

"Why?"

"No reason," he said. "You just look pretty with your hair down is all."

She had to turn away so he didn't see her blush.

Unfortunately, she turned straight toward the mirror and caught him looking at her. She tugged the hat over her long waves, tucked her hair behind her ears, and faced him.

"Oh, never mind," he said. "Now you look downright gorgeous."

Her breath caught in her throat. Why did he have to make pretending she didn't love him so darn hard? She rolled her eyes, for effect. "Let's go."

They stepped out into the night, enveloped by cold and lit only by the faint glow of the moon. There was something romantic about Christmas on Nantucket, not that she'd ever had the opportunity to partake in that romance herself.

She fell into step beside him, and they were quiet as they walked.

"I forgot what it's like here in the winter," he said. "Peaceful."

"I love the quiet."

"Then I won't mess it up by talking." He laughed.

She bumped him with her shoulder and smiled at him. Her smile faded around the same time his did. "Are you ever going to tell me what's going on?"

He frowned. "What do you mean?"

"I know you, Hayes," she said. "I know when you're faking it."

He stopped her, then pointed to the sidewalk where a small patch of ice stretched out in her path. He took her hand and led her to the other side, around the ice, and then kept on walking, like it was the most normal thing in the world.

And maybe it was. Maybe that was simply how Hayes

McGuire treated people. She'd decided a long time ago that his casual relationships with women meant something about him, but she realized in that moment it was an unfair assumption.

"I'm not faking anything," he said.

"Did you know there are two versions of Hayes McGuire?" she said with authority. "There's genuine Hayes. He smiles all the way through his eyes. He's warm and kind and deflects praise. He doesn't want to talk about himself but will regale you with stories of his travels if he thinks it might make you smile."

A smile crawled across his face as he stared straight ahead.

"Then there's this Hayes. His smile stops at his lips, and there's something slightly troubled behind his eyes. Like he's wrestling with something he doesn't want to talk about. Or making a decision he doesn't have the answer to."

He looked at her. "You've got this all wrong, Pru. I'm just weirded out that my aunt wants me to play matchmaker while she runs off to Paris with her husband."

They were on Main Street now, coming in to the crowd. Rosy-cheeked children passed by, squealing in delight at the sights and sounds unfolding around them. They stopped to maneuver around the line at a quaint stand selling hot chocolate.

Soon, the Town Crier would emerge, counting down to the tree lighting and caroling ceremony, signaling the start of the Christmas season. At his pronouncement, over 150 balsam trees lining the cobblestoned Nantucket streets would magically light up as part of the Christmas Stroll.

"My parents are close to the front," Hayes said now. "They wanted a good view of your tree." He took her hand and led her through the chattering crowd, until finally they located the McGuire clan.

"You made it," Hayes's mom said as he and Pru squeezed in beside the rest of them. She gave Pru a quick hug. "Good to see you, hon. The tree is beautiful. So fun."

She always made Pru feel so loved. "Good to see you too."

The crowd stilled as the head of the Nantucket Chamber called for their attention. Behind him was the tree Pru had decorated with mini surfboard ornaments she'd made by hand. She'd kept a summery color palette and a lot of pink and blue lights, and in just a few minutes, it would illuminate Main Street. The following Saturday, it would talk.

Maybe it *was* a big deal. Pru certainly felt special having Hayes and his family there to celebrate with her.

Pru glanced over at Hayes, who watched in silence, but seemed to be somewhere else entirely.

"You okay?" she whispered as the man speaking handed the microphone off to the Town Crier.

He glanced down at her and frowned. "I told you, I'm fine." He nudged her with his shoulder. "Stop worrying."

"Now, join me as we count down together!" the Town Crier said loudly.

They all counted down from ten, and when they reached one, the dimly lit street turned bright white, filled with the magic of Christmas. The crowd gasped in response as the high school's a cappella group began to sing "Joy to the World."

The McGuire family sang along with excited fervor,

but after a minute or two, Pru noticed Hayes's enthusiasm waned, and she was more certain than ever that something was bothering him. He must've noticed her watching him because he quickly started up again, grinning a little too widely.

She shoved her worry aside and joined in, their voices ringing out in the chilly night air. They sang several more traditional Christmas carols, and Pru couldn't help but savor the moment. It had been so long since she'd spent the holidays with friends who felt like family.

At the end of the evening, they said their goodbyes, and she and Hayes started the walk back to her cottage. Once they were away from the crowd, she stopped.

He took a few steps before realizing it, then turned back to look at her. "What's wrong?"

"Hayes, I know it's been a while since you saw me in person, but I'm still the same old Prudence. And I know you better than anybody."

"I know, Pru." He took a step toward her.

"So, I know if you're not telling me what's going on, you're not telling anyone."

He looked away.

She took his hand. She wanted to press a kiss to his palm but decided that was a tiny bit over the line of friendship. Instead, she squeezed it and forced his gaze. "You can talk to me, okay?"

He didn't move. For a moment, it seemed like he wasn't even breathing. Then, finally, he nodded. "When I'm ready."

She shoved away her disappointment that he didn't instantly trust her with whatever it was he battled, but gave him one quick nod "I'll be here when you are."

CHAPTER 5

THE RULES

*H*ow did she do that? How did she, unlike everyone else in the world, read him like he had his emotional life's story written on his face?

Hayes had tried to pretend everything was fine. He'd tried to pretend he wasn't haunted by the images that kept him awake at night, that he was unfazed. He'd been pretending for almost three months now.

But Pru had still seen through him.

Nobody else had. Only her. He supposed that's why she was his best friend. Still, he couldn't talk about it. He knew she wouldn't forget, that she'd always be wondering until the day he told her—which may be never—maybe he would just get over it and the joy would return to his eyes or whatever had to happen to make her think he was okay.

He was Hayes McGuire. He was always okay. This time would be no different.

Unless it was.

Now, after hours of standing out in the cold, warmed

from the inside by the mulled cider, they walked back to her cottage in the darkness.

The island was perfectly safe, and still, he found himself inching closer to Pru, as if she needed to be protected from something unknown.

From something he'd witnessed but couldn't process.

When really, he was the one in need of a safe haven.

"So, what are the rules?" she asked now as they rounded the corner onto her street.

He stuffed his hands in his coat pockets and wished he'd brought a pair of gloves. It was stupid of him not to. A chill raced down his back. "The rules of what?"

"Noni Rose," she said with a knowing smile.

"You're gonna help me?"

She shrugged. "I gave it some thought in between the fifth and sixth verses of 'Silent Night.'"

He grinned at her. "I knew you couldn't resist."

"I can't leave poor Peggy Swinton in your hands. I don't know what Aunt Nellie was thinking, you're the least romantic person I know."

"Thank God," he said. "I could kiss you right now." Oh, heck. Where had that come from? "I mean, I'm thankful. Very thankful."

Her eyes had widened when he said it. It was barely detectable, but he'd noticed. It was there. That was such a stupid thing to say. A great way to make things awkward and run her off.

Idiot!

"And I resent the fact that you think I'm not romantic," he said. "I'm plenty romantic."

She looked straight ahead and muttered a nearly silent, "Uh-huh."

They reached her front door, and she pulled out her key, opened the lock, and led him inside. The box sat on the table where they'd left it. Inside was his future as a *matchmaker.*

If Hollis or his dad or any of his friends ever found out about this . . .

"The first thing we need is an oath of silence," he said.

She stood at the stove, where he only now realized she'd put a kettle on to boil. He'd forgotten how much she loved hot cocoa. Even in the summer, she drank it extra hot with a dollop of whipped cream.

"I see you eyeing my kettle," she said.

"I was doing no such thing."

She raised a brow. "So many lies tonight, Mr. McGuire. I know how you feel about my hot cocoa."

He took off his coat. "I feel absolutely indifferent about this drink."

"Lies."

He plopped down on the couch. "I'm not sleeping very well."

From behind him, he heard her clinking around in the kitchen, pulling the whipped cream from the fridge, finding mugs and spoons. She stopped. "Yeah?"

He started to remember, and in seconds, he was back there—a world away. A heartbeat away.

"How long's it been since you had a good night of sleep?"

He leaned forward, elbows on his knees, head in his hands. "Months." The nightmares always woke him, and once he was awake, he didn't go back to sleep. Usually, that meant the hours of 3:00 a.m. to 6:00 a.m. were spent staring at the ceiling.

She handed him a mug of hot chocolate, filled to the rim with whipped cream, crushed peppermint sprinkled on top, then sat on the opposite end of the couch.

"Ooh, the peppermint is new," he said.

"What can I say? I do it up fancy." She waggled her eyebrows. Man, she was pretty.

He took a drink, letting it warm him from the inside out. "That's so good."

She set her mug on the table, pulled her legs up underneath her, and spread a blanket over her lap. Then, she took her mug, settled it between her hands, and looked at him as if to say, *You have my full attention.*

And yet, she said nothing. It was as if she wanted him to know she was there without forcing herself on him. He loved her for that.

"Anyway," he said. "Noni Rose."

Disappointment skittered across her face, but she quickly recovered. He knew he was letting her down by keeping it all bottled up, but he just wasn't ready —not yet.

He set his drink down and picked up the box. "Let's go over the rules. Maybe then we can come up with a plan."

Inside the box, right on top, was a small notebook. Aunt Nellie had gone over most of it with him, but already, he could use a refresher. Truth be told, he was only half-listening because at the time, he expected his aunt to realize what a crazy idea this was and tell him to forget the whole thing.

How had things gotten so turned around?

He opened the old, discolored notebook and read: "Rule Number One: The matchmaker must never reveal that she is making a match."

He stopped and looked at Pru. "Already, I have evidence that this is not a man's job."

Pru smiled, took another sip of her drink, and nodded toward the book.

"Rule Number Two: The matchmaker cannot force a match. She may see what she thinks is a perfect pairing, but matchmakers are human, and sometimes humanity gets in the way of the magic." Hayes looked at Pru, wearing his best *you've got to be kidding me* expression.

"You're really not selling this," she said.

"No? I thought I was basically a walking infomercial over here." He tossed her an eye roll, and she snatched the notebook out of his hand.

"Okay, it goes on to say that once a matchmaker selects her target, she should take time to observe the target in his or her natural habitat."

"Are we zoologists now?" He shook his head. "Do I need to write a report on the feeding and sleeping habits of Peggy Swinton?"

She laughed. "It says, 'Do not dream up a wish list of potential matches. Rather, go where the target is and wait for the magic to reveal itself to you.'"

When Prudence looked up from the notebook, Hayes made a point to roll his eyes again. "This is insane."

She shrugged. "I mean, you saw the book with all the success stories in it. Maybe the rules work."

"Don't tell me you're buying in to all of this."

She ignored him and gave her attention back to the notebook. "Rule Number Three," she said. "The matchmaker must never attempt to match someone whose heart has already been given away." Her eyes darted up over the notebook and she found him watching her.

A strange, awkward moment passed between them, and then she tossed the notebook on the couch. "You're right. They take this really seriously."

"That's what I'm saying," Hayes said. "Are we really going to go stalk Peggy until some magical man materializes out of nowhere?"

Pru stilled.

"What is it?"

She shrugged. "I know you don't live here, but do you know Peggy Swinton?"

"Not really," he said. "I mean, I've talked to her a couple of times over the years."

The look on Pru's face turned thoughtful. "I think she's one of the nicest people I've ever met. Inherently kind, you know, not someone who has to try to be nice. She's really involved in the Nantucket Historical Society, and she's taught third grade for over thirty years."

"Never married?"

Pru shook her head. "There was a rumor a few years back that she was engaged once, a long time ago. I wonder if she just had her heart broken and chose not to put herself through that again."

Hayes looked away. He knew a little something about that. "Well, it can be hard to put yourself out there when you know what you're risking."

She nodded. "I know."

But did she? Far as he knew, Pru had never really given her heart to anyone. "Must've been some broken heart if she never tried again."

"Or maybe she never stopped loving whoever it was?" Pru picked her mug back up. "I mean, if it was real, maybe she's hoping he'll find his way back?"

Hayes frowned. "That would be crazy."

A smile played at the corners of her lips. "Why? Because you can't imagine loving one woman that much?"

He rolled his eyes. "Because there's not just one person for everyone."

Her brow knit into a tight line. "Is that right?"

He leaned back on the couch but didn't respond.

"Then why haven't you settled down?" she asked. "If any old woman would do, why not pick one and make it official?"

They didn't talk much about the women he dated. Occasionally, Pru made a remark that let him know she had opinions on his love life, but it was a topic they mostly avoided, though he wasn't sure why. Same with her love life—if she'd ever fallen in love, she certainly hadn't told him about it.

And yet, he felt so close to her. She was maybe his only true friend other than Hollis. How could that be when there was such a big part of their lives that seemed to be off-limits for discussion?

She looked away. "Unlike you, I do believe there's one person for everyone."

"Like a soulmate," he said, thinking back to his conversation with Aunt Nellie.

She found his eyes again. "Yeah, like a soulmate."

Something inexplicable passed between them. Something he hadn't felt before. He remembered the first time he ever saw Pru, riding a wave that had taken him out at the knees. She was so confident, so stunning, he'd asked her out then and there. Before Delilah. Before Kara. Before every other leggy blonde that had found her way onto his arm.

And she put him in his place—hard. It made her that much more interesting to him, but it was clear by their next encounter she had no interest in dating him, so they became friends. She taught him to surf a whole lot better that summer, and when he left the island at the end of the season, they stayed in touch.

He'd never been friends with a woman before, not like this. And it was nice. And while they never got into the nitty-gritty of his relationships, she gave him insights into the way the female mind worked. Never mind that most female minds he encountered didn't seem to work like Pru's.

She was different. Special. He supposed that's why they'd stayed friends when all of his other relationships fizzled out before they ever began. And that's why they were nothing more. He wasn't worthy of Prudence Sutton, though at that moment he wondered if any man was.

"I never took you for a romantic," he said.

She smiled, turning the air between them light again. "There's a lot you don't know about me, Mr. McGuire." She poked his thigh with her foot, playfully.

That simple connection between them changed the mood in an instant.

"What else?" She nodded toward the notebook.

He picked it up and flipped to the next page. "There's more."

She took a sip and set her mug down, then wrapped her arms around her knees. "I'm listening."

"It's a letter." He read it out loud while Pru sat in silence.

. . .

Dear Noni Rose,

This is a great responsibility, and one you must treat with the utmost care and consideration. Any time matters of the heart collide with a person's entire future, it's not to be taken lightly. You have been chosen, not by a person but by the matchmaker's magic, which will, whether you believe it or not, also come to you when you need it most. You see, matchmaking is not for the faint of heart. You may have some bumps along the way. But when you pause and let the magic work and you learn to trust yourself a little, wonderful things can happen.

There is nothing better than seeing how perfect two people are for each other and then giving them the proper nudge so they can figure it out for themselves. If you're asking why you have been selected for this task—if you're thinking this isn't something you'll be good at, you're not alone. Every Noni Rose before you has felt the same. But let me assure you, the magic has chosen you. Like a sprinkle of fairy dust.

Best of luck to you.

Magically yours,

Noni Rose

WHEN HE FINISHED, he closed the notebook and set it on the table. "So, you'll help me?"

"Exactly how do you want me to help?"

"Help me find Peggy Swinton's soulmate."

Her face brightened into a wide grin. "There's hope for you yet, my friend."

"Well, don't tell anyone," he said. "I've got a reputation to protect."

She laughed. "You and me both. I can't have the guys

who come into the shop thinking I've gone soft. I'll lose all credibility."

And just like that, the easy banter was back.

But as he lay in bed that night, staring at the ceiling, it wasn't the banter that he replayed in his mind. It was the strange shift between them when they were talking about soulmates and the faint, nagging question that asked if maybe he'd already found his.

CHAPTER 6

PANCAKES AND BACON

*P*rudence Sutton had not gone soft. She was not now, nor would she ever be, the kind of hopeless romantic who made poor decisions. She'd built her business on relationships with men who regularly hit on her, and the only way she'd done that was to prove to them she wasn't going to go weak in the knees because they told her she was pretty.

Why, then, did she see the need to admit she was holding out for a *soulmate* to the one person she believed might actually *be* her soulmate?

Stupid. Stupid. Stupid.

She had a feeling that conversation was going to get brought up again, probably in the form of mockery, and she'd regretted it the second she said it. Hayes, like the guys in the surf shop, had an opinion about her—and that opinion kept her cover intact. An opinion that said Prudence Sutton had no interest in romance.

It kept him from ever suspecting she would even think of wanting anything other than friendship with him.

It's why they worked.

If they were going to spend the next couple of weeks together, she was going to have to be more careful. Otherwise, she'd spook him, and the very thing she was trying to prevent would happen—he'd deem their relationship "too complicated," and she'd go the way of the rest of the women in his life.

Why had she agreed to this? Matchmaking Peggy was one thing, but doing it with Hayes was something else entirely. They were bound to have conversations about what made two people compatible—how was she supposed to play it cool then?

The knock on her door forced her to stop thinking crazy. Seconds later, Hayes's beautiful face appeared in her entryway.

She looked up from the stove, where she stood making pancakes and bacon, and flashed him a *we're just friends* smile.

"You're cooking," he said.

"I figured we needed some sustenance to get us through the day," she said.

He strode toward her, picked up a piece of bacon from the napkin on the counter, broke it in half, and popped a piece in his mouth. "Yeah, matchmaking is bound to take it out of us."

She gave him a shove, and only then did she take a moment to look him in the face. His eyes were drawn, his skin pale. "Did you sleep last night?"

He ate the other half of his bacon and poured himself a cup of coffee. "Sure. About three hours."

She turned off the burner and carried a plate of pancakes to the table. "Three hours?"

He set his mug down at the place she'd set for him, a place where he'd eaten a hundred times before. There was nothing more special or intimate about this time—so why did it feel like there was?

Wishful thinking . . . ?

Yes, her imagination did have a way of running off on its own, especially where Hayes was concerned.

"I told you I don't sleep well," he said.

"Yeah, but you didn't tell me why." She topped off her own cup of coffee, added peppermint creamer and stirred, watching the colors meld together to form the perfect shade of brown.

He inhaled, then let out a sigh.

"Not yet?" she asked.

He found her eyes and shook his head.

"Let's eat." She couldn't push. Whatever this was that was bothering him, it was big enough to steal something from Hayes that made him who he was. That joyful, outgoing personality he'd always possessed had been doused by something he didn't want to talk about.

What if he'd had his heart broken? What if one of his casual relationships had actually meant more to him than he'd let on?

If that was the case, it was better that he stayed quiet. She wasn't sure she wanted to know.

"So, we should get a plan," she said.

"Right." He poured a ridiculous amount of syrup over his buttered pancakes.

She quirked a brow, nodding at his plate.

"What?"

"Do you think you've got enough syrup?"

He picked up the bottle, turned it over, and squeezed another circle onto his plate. "Now I do."

She shook her head. "You're like a twelve-year-old boy." If only that made him less—and not more—adorable. These childlike qualities only endeared her to him, and she hated that.

"Maybe we should talk about Peggy," Pru said, desperately needing a mental subject change.

"So, we're actually doing this." He said it like a statement, not a question.

She stopped mid-bite. "Didn't we say we were?"

"Yeah," he said. "It's just so bizarre. And Aunt Nellie left for Paris today. What would she have done if I'd said no?"

Pru grinned. "She knew you wouldn't say no. She flattered you into saying yes."

"You think I'm that easy?" he asked. "That a little flattery will make me do something I'm morally opposed to?"

"Morally opposed?" She took a bite. Her pancakes were perfect today. She wouldn't let on that she'd tried extra hard. And she certainly wouldn't show him the pile of burnt ones that had landed in the garbage can. "Why?"

He ate another piece of bacon. Oh, to be a man and eat bacon like it was fruit. "I just don't think this is how it works. It's like online dating—not natural."

"That's easy for you to say."

"You think so?"

"Sure," she said. "First, you're a good-looking single guy, which already puts you at an advantage. Second, you're good with people, so you have no problem meeting women. But for someone like Peggy Swinton, that's not reality."

"You think I'm good-looking?" He grinned.

She rolled her eyes. "Is that all you heard?"

He shrugged. "I've learned to filter out what's not important."

"You're right, it's weird Aunt Nellie picked you as her replacement." She took another bite. "You know nothing about the plight of the single woman."

"So, tell me."

Heat rushed to her cheeks. "No."

"No, really," he said. "I want to hear about your plight."

She squinted at him. "Why do you sound skeptical?"

"Because I don't believe you suffer any kind of *plight.*" He chewed another bite, swallowed, then raised his eyebrows, waiting for her reply. "I think you could have any guy you wanted."

She knew it was her turn for a witty retort, but her mind had gone blank.

His smile wasn't helping her focus.

Finally, words returned. "Well, good men are typically harder to find than good women," she said. "So, we already have that working against us. It's like men are genetically dispositioned to not seek out meaningful relationships, whereas women are."

He frowned. "That's a little stereotypical, don't you think?"

"I'm just trying to explain why someone good and kind like Peggy can't find a decent man."

"I thought we were looking for her soulmate."

She knew that would be back to bite her. "Take the soulmate out of the equation."

"Because you know it doesn't exist?"

"No," she said. "Because we're just talking about dating right now."

"Okay, so what about you?" He shoveled a stack of pancake onto his fork.

"What about me?"

"If women are created to seek out meaningful relationships, why are you still single?"

She picked up her mug and did her best to avoid his gaze. Her best wasn't good enough. Nothing could've withstood the magnetic pull of Hayes's hazel eyes. "I'm not a good case study. I think more like a guy."

"So, you don't want a meaningful relationship." His tone turned casual. "A *soulmate*."

His emphasis on that word was very effective.

"That's not what I said." She didn't like this conversation one little bit.

"But you haven't had a meaningful relationship for as long as I've known you," he said. "I mean, I remember you dating a few different guys, but after about two months, you were single again."

"With one exception, we have that in common."

He sipped his coffee, seemingly unfazed by her attempt to steer the conversation.

"What's your point?" She asked, much more flustered than she should be.

"I'm just trying to debunk your theory here," he said.

"Well, we're not talking about me," she said, wishing they actually weren't talking about her. "We're talking about Peggy."

"Okay," he said. "So why has it been hard for Peggy to find a good partner?"

She chewed her mouthful, swallowed, and pushed her plate away. "Other than the rumor she was engaged once, I don't know that much about her. She's on the committee for the Festival of Trees, though."

"So, she'll be at the preview party?" he asked.

She nodded.

"The one where they're honoring you?"

Another nod.

"Perfect."

She frowned. "Why perfect?"

"You can talk to her."

"Me?" She didn't like the sound of that. When it came to people, Hayes was much better at conversation.

"Sure, you're both single women, you'll have a lot to chat about." He ate his last bite. "You can swap stories about soulmates and meaningful relationships."

She narrowed her gaze. "You are the matchmaker here. I'm not doing all the work for you."

"I will scout out potential male prospects," he said. "I'll wait for that tingly, magical feeling. I'm sure it's like a radar or something."

"I don't know if that's how it works." She stood, picked up her plate, and reached for his.

He held up a hand. "Nope. Sit. You cooked, so I'll clean."

"You're my guest," she said.

He rolled his eyes. "I'm practically family. Sit down."

She did as she was told, begrudging the fact that he'd reminded her that he thought of her like another sister.

"So, we have a plan?" he said, pulling her attention.

"I guess so," she said. "Though I don't know how sound it is."

"That's okay," he said. "Why don't we go out and see if we can observe Peggy in her natural habitat?"

She laughed. "Fine. Let's go see if we can find her."

CHAPTER 7

GUT FEELINGS

They arrived at the Nantucket Whaling Museum after a short drive from Pru's little cottage. He was grateful she let him drive her SUV this time—she still remembered how much he hated to be the passenger.

Hayes liked to be the one behind the wheel. In control. Which was probably why he was still so bothered by his last freelance assignment. So bothered he'd yet to accept another one. At some point, he was going to have to face that. Sure, he'd found a number of various income streams, but they wouldn't last forever. Eventually, the guy who'd built a whole brand around travel was going to have to travel again.

"You think she's here?" he asked as they got out of the car and walked toward the entrance.

Pru shrugged. "It's the only place I know to look. She's pretty involved on the committee, and I know they've got a lot of work to do before the festival next weekend."

He pulled the door open and followed her inside. In just a few days, the preview party would be held here, and

Hayes would return to Nantucket society after an extended absence. Odd that it had been only a few short months since summer. With all that had happened, it felt like a lifetime had gone by.

They walked up the stairs and into the room that was being decorated for Thursday's event.

In true Prudence fashion, she'd agreed to not only decorate the twenty-foot tall talking tree on Main Street, but also a smaller version of the same thing here in the whaling museum as part of the Festival of Trees. She'd finished her trees days ago. Unlike everyone else he knew, Pru didn't procrastinate, except, it seemed, when it came to finding a meaningful relationship.

As they walked toward the back where he assumed her tree was located, he watched the way she moved. Graceful, yet strong, which was an interesting combination. Interesting and unique. He was pretty sure that when it came to Prudence Sutton, he'd been let in to a very small inner circle.

How many people knew she'd grown up in a trailer park with a mother who worked as a waitress in a local dive bar and a stepfather who turned mean and handsy when he got drunk? How many people knew she'd come here the summer after she graduated high school, found a job at the surf shop, and never went back?

How many people knew she never touched alcohol or that she blasted eighties music and danced around her living room to try and shake her sadness off?

"So, what would you say *is* your most meaningful relationship?" he asked, aware that his smirk would keep things light between them. That's where the magic of their friendship seemed to exist—in this familiar flirtatious chitchat they both excelled at.

"Are you still on this?" she asked, weaving around partially decorated Christmas trees.

"I mean, I'm curious," he said.

"Are you asking me present tense what my most meaningful relationship is?" she asked.

He shrugged. "Sure, I guess."

She squinted, as if trying to decide between a great number of contenders. "I think my most meaningful relationship—the one I couldn't do without—" Her eyes searched the ceiling. Then, like a light bulb going off, she brought her gaze to his. "Definitely Anton, my favorite barista at Nantucket Bean." She grinned at him.

"It's me," he said. "You don't have to tell me."

She stopped short and ducked behind a partially decorated Christmas tree. "It's Peggy."

"Peggy is your most meaningful relationship?"

She gave his arm a tug and pointed across the room. "No, it's Peggy."

"Why are you hiding?"

Her eyes darted from one side to the other, and then she straightened her shoulders and smoothed her hands on her pants. "I'm not."

"And you're whispering," he whispered. "This is matchmaking, not espionage."

She gave him a shove and emerged from behind the tree. "I don't like you."

He grinned. "No, you love me."

She straightened, then walked off, and he followed, eyes glued to the older woman decorating one of the trees in the corner.

"I didn't know you were decorating a tree," Pru said when they reached her.

"Oh, Miss Sutton." Peggy's cheeks flushed pink. "I didn't expect to see you here. Your tree is so beautiful. I admit I wasn't sure how surfboards and Christmas went together, but you really pulled it off."

Pru smiled graciously. "Thank you, Miss Swinton."

"Call me Peggy."

"Only if you call me Prudence."

Aunt Nellie might've selected Hayes to be her stand-in Noni Rose, but he'd been smart to enlist Pru's help. She was every bit as good with people as he was. Peggy, who seemed shy and a little mousy, positively beamed in her presence.

"Peggy, you remember Hayes McGuire?" Pru put a hand on his arm, which sent a strange sensation straight down to his toes.

What in the world?

Peggy turned to him. "I do indeed. You're all grown up, Mr. McGuire."

"If we're all on a first-name basis here, you're going to have to call me Hayes."

Peggy smiled. "I'm here putting the finishing touches on the library's tree."

He glanced at the Christmas tree beside her and saw the decorations had been made entirely out of book pages.

"It looks beautiful," Pru said.

"Is that the famous surfboard artist, Miss Prudence Sutton?"

They all turned in the direction of a man's voice. When Prudence spotted the older, Jimmy Buffett lookalike, she let out a squeal like he'd never heard. Hayes took a step back while Prudence threw herself in the man's arms. He glanced over at Peggy, who had turned so red she might as well be a sun-ripened tomato.

"Hayes, you remember Howie!" Pru hugged him again, then squeezed his arm.

"Oh, right." Hayes shook the man's hand. "You used to own the surf shop."

"Before he sold it to me." Pru's entire face brightened. "This man taught me everything I know about making surfboards, and a few things I never wanted to know about drinking tequila—namely, don't do it." She laughed.

As Pru chattered on, Hayes stole quick glances at Peggy, who seemed unable to decide if she should stick around for a conversation she wasn't really a part of or take off—which he suspected was what she'd rather do.

But there was something else too. Her cheeks were still flushed, and she refused to look at Howie.

He glanced over at Howie, whose attention seemed to be split between Prudence and Peggy.

"I can't believe you're here," Pru said now.

"Howie, do you remember Peggy Swinton?" Hayes asked.

Pru glanced at him, then realized she'd been blabbering on—and while it was adorable, it was slightly rude to poor Peggy, who looked like she might explode.

Howie reached out and took Peggy's hand, not quite a handshake. "Peggy."

The older woman still refused his eyes. She pulled her hand away. "I just remembered I have a very important errand to run."

Pru frowned as Peggy raced off, drawing Howie's undivided attention.

A slight tingle chased itself down Hayes's spine. He looked at Peggy, then at Howie, and there was the tingle again.

Magic.

Oh, crap.

"That was strange," Prudence said, turning back to Howie.

Howie shrugged.

"So, you're in town for the holidays?" Hayes asked.

"Had to come see this tree Prudence designed," he said. "It's not every year a surfboard artist gets to design the talking tree."

Pru's cheeks turned the faintest shade of pink. "I'm glad you're back."

"Wouldn't have missed it," Howie said. "Can I take you both to lunch?"

Personally, Hayes was still full of pancakes, but he had a feeling their day had just been mapped out for them. Howie meant a lot to Pru. While Hayes left at the end of the summers, Nantucket native Howie Basford hung around the island all year round. He was the reason Prudence chose to live here. He taught her a trade when college was too expensive. She had a lot of reasons to love the guy.

And when he left the island five years ago, after a bitter divorce from a woman no one in town had ever really liked, he sold the surf shop to Prudence. Because of him, she had a good life and a career she could be proud of. She'd never said so, but Howie was the closest thing to a father Pru had ever had.

"Maybe I should see if I can find Peggy," Hayes said. "You two go catch up."

Pru looked at him, her eyes wide. "Oh, right. Peggy."

"Something wrong with Peggy?" Howie asked.

"Other than the way she dashed out of here like she'd seen a ghost," Pru said, "no."

"I'll see if I can help her out with the rest of the preparations here," Hayes said. "We'll meet up later, Pru?"

She nodded, then glanced at Howie. "Shall we?"

And as much as Hayes didn't want to be Nantucket's matchmaker, he had a gut feeling he couldn't ignore.

Peggy Swinton was about to be matched.

CHAPTER 8

THAT SHIP HAS SAILED

"Still carrying that torch, I see." Howie leaned back in the sprawling booth of a quiet Nantucket bistro right downtown.

Pru scoffed. "What are you talking about?"

Howie quirked a brow in her direction, and she knew there was no point pretending with him. He'd always been able to read her like a book.

"Is it that obvious?"

The waitress brought their drinks and Pru stuck a straw in her Cherry Coke and took a drink.

"Those straws are killing the turtles." Howie nodded toward her drink.

She glanced up and found him watching her, his unwrapped straw still sitting on the table. She pulled the straw out and set it on her napkin. "Happy?"

"Indeed."

Howie talked a lot like the surfers who came in from California. Not a drawl, but a slow cadence that would've likely lulled her to sleep if she weren't on high alert thanks to his unwanted observations.

"And to answer your question," he said, "yes, it is that obvious. At least to me. He seems oblivious though."

She sighed. "Or he knows, and he pretends not to. Probably doesn't want to have to let me down easy."

"Maybe," Howie said. "At least he knows a good thing when he sees it."

She rolled her eyes. Hayes might know a good thing, but he didn't want it—not for himself.

"Have you told him how you feel?" He picked up his glass and took a drink.

She shook her head. "I can't risk losing him. He's my—"

"Best friend," he interrupted. "I know. You've been saying that for a lot of years."

"Well, it's true."

"It's also a great excuse not to put yourself out there."

She narrowed her gaze, thinking it felt strange to see him in anything other than an unbuttoned Hawaiian shirt and board shorts. He was out of place in his full-length pants and gray sweater. Somehow, he was still that same bronze color he was in the summer. She supposed that's what happened when you spent your retirement hopping around various sun-filled islands.

"What about you?" she asked.

"What about me?"

"You put yourself out there?"

He sighed. The waitress reappeared, sliding loaded plates on the table. When they told her they didn't need anything else, she disappeared. Pru's question and Howie's sigh still hung in the air.

"Well?" She picked up her sandwich, aware that there was no way she would finish this meal after such a large breakfast. And for a fleeting moment, she wondered what Hayes was doing right now.

"You know I put myself out there plenty," he said. "Bit me in the keister. I'm happy on my own."

Howie had been married to a woman named Tammy who had frizzy hair and a permanent scowl. Pru used to be offended that Tammy didn't like her until Nantucket locals told her Tammy didn't like anybody. Not even Howie, it seemed.

She'd married Howie before he quit business school in favor of a life on the beach, and she'd never accepted his surf shop as a legitimate business. Never mind that Howie was smart enough to invest his profits. Now, the man had plenty of money to spend his retirement exactly how he wanted—on the beach.

Howie had sold Pru the surf shop for a dollar, making it clear the only thing he wanted in return was for her to have a happy life.

Was she living up to her end of the deal?

"Don't you think maybe there's someone else out there for you?" Pru asked him now.

Howie's face was weather-worn and leathery. His blue eyes still shone bright, and while she knew he was in his early sixties, she also knew he had a big heart and a lot of love yet to give.

He popped a French fry in his mouth and chewed. "Maybe it's crossed my mind."

"Yeah?" She grinned. "You know what they say about Christmas in Nantucket."

He frowned. "It's cold?"

"It's magical," she said. "Maybe you'll meet someone at the Stroll."

He shook his head. "How'd we get to talking about me, Pru? We should be devising a plan to get that boy to realize what we already know."

"Oh, and what's that?"

"That you are the best thing that's ever happened to him." Howie waggled his eyebrows.

"Promise me you will not say a word, Howie," she said. "This is the one time you don't know better than me."

He took a bite of his sandwich, then swiped his napkin across his smug mouth.

"Howie."

"Fine," he said. "I won't say anything. But take it from me, Pru, you should. Or time will march on, and you'll look back with nothing but a pile of regret."

And as the conversation turned to happier topics, she had to wonder what exactly he regretted, because the warning certainly sounded like one that came from experience.

HAYES FOUND Peggy underneath the hanging whale bones on the main floor of the museum. She seemed to be putting the finishing touches on another tree.

"Miss Swinton?" he said as he approached.

She turned. Had she been crying? Her red eyes were puffy, but she affixed a smile in place and pretended otherwise. "Oh, you didn't leave with your girlfriend?"

He put a hand up. "Pru's just a friend."

"Ahh," she said. "I'm sorry, I just assumed."

"It happens." He smiled at her. "Are you okay?"

"Oh, I'm fine, but it's sweet of you to ask." She waved him off and turned back to the tree. Peggy was the epitome of a third-grade teacher. She was kind and sweet—overly so, really. And while he didn't know much about the woman, he did know that she loved Nantucket, and she was good with kids. So good, in fact, that Hayes thought it was a shame she'd never had any of her own.

Maybe that's why she'd been crying.

No. He had a gut feeling it was something (or someone) else entirely. Aunt Nellie was right—there was a tingle, the magic.

"You don't seem fine," Hayes said. "You seem kind of upset."

She hesitated for a beat, then hung a gold ornament on the tree. "Truth be told, I used to be somebody's Prudence."

"What do you mean?' He glanced down at a plastic bin holding ornaments and bows. "May I?"

She nodded, giving him permission to help her decorate. "Oh, it's nothing. Nothing a young, good-looking boy like you would want to hear about anyway."

He flashed her the smile that always served him well, though he'd never tried to win over someone like Peggy. "Try me."

Maybe it was the Noni Rose magic, or maybe Nellie was right and people *did* open up to Hayes, or maybe it was his flirtatious grin—whatever it was, Peggy drew in a deep breath, moved to the other side of the tree, and cleared her throat.

"It was a lifetime ago," she said. "There was a boy who

was a very good friend of mine. We were inseparable, really—a lot like you and Prudence, I gather."

He continued to add ornaments to the tree, careful not to interrupt her. After all, if he was going to be successful with this matchmaking thing, he needed to know Peggy's story. It was part of observing her in her natural habitat, he supposed.

"I thought one day we might end up together." She moved behind the tree to work on the opposite side. "You know, romantically. Things were always so easy between us. I've always thought the best relationships were the ones that started as friendships." She popped her head around the tree and looked at him. "That's some free advice for you, young man."

"Much appreciated." He chuckled. "So, what happened?"

"It's a long story," she said. "But the short of it is—he married my best friend."

Hayes stilled. Even now, all these years later, he could see the pain behind Peggy's eyes.

"He and I were so close, but neither one of us had made a move, I guess you'd say. And, well, she did."

"But you loved him," he said.

Peggy nodded sadly.

"And she knew it."

Another nod. "That didn't stop her from asking me to be her maid of honor."

"Wow, that's cold."

Peggy sighed. "Our friendship didn't last very long after that."

"And the guy?"

She disappeared behind the tree again. "His wife

demanded that he stop being friends with me. And that's what he did."

Hayes tossed a bow back into the bin and moved around the other side of the Christmas tree. "Peggy, I'm really sorry that happened to you."

She reached over and took his hand. "I don't like to talk about it, but I share it with you as a cautionary tale."

He frowned. "How so?"

"You and Miss Prudence. You remind me a lot of me and that boy. Don't wait until it's too late."

"Like I said before, Peggy, Pru and I are just friends."

"All I know—and I don't know much—is that she looks at you the way I looked at him. Don't wait until someone else tells her how he feels about her. You could lose her forever." She squeezed his hand, then bent over and picked up the bin. "Now, I should get going. It was really nice talking to you, Mr. McGuire."

She started off in the opposite direction.

"Peggy?" he called after her.

She turned, eyes wide in reply.

"Maybe it's not too late?"

She scoffed. "No, that ship has sailed. But you're sweet to say so." She walked away, leaving Hayes standing in the warm glow of the white lights.

CHAPTER 9

PRUDENCE, MEANING "CAUTIOUS"

*T*he ceiling was still the same shade of gray it had been when Pru went to bed hours ago. She knew because she couldn't stop staring at it. A streetlamp cast a shadow through the window, and if she rolled over, she'd have a bird's-eye view of her entire cottage.

Her whole world, right there in that house.

Only, that wasn't true, was it? Her world was scattered all over Nantucket at the moment. Her surf shop. Her friends. Howie.

Hayes.

Having Howie back in town was definitely a good thing—except for the fact that the man could see right through her. Had he always known how she felt about Hayes? She'd never admitted it to anyone before.

The minutes ticked by, and Pru tossed and turned, wishing she could take back her conversation with Howie —because now that the truth was out there, floating around the magical Christmas air of Nantucket—it was far more likely to land on the wrong pair of ears.

She groaned. Rolled over. Punched her pillow. Then tried to think of all the reasons she and Hayes were a terrible match.

Their friendship had come easily. After she turned him down at the beach the day they met, she saw him out at a party a few nights later. Thanks to her disaster of a stepfather, Pru never drank, but she wanted to get out and meet people, so she let an acquaintance twist her arm and she found herself on the back deck of some rich guy's cottage.

And there, in the yard, was the guy from the beach. She watched him, this confident mystery man, as he made the rounds, talking to everyone there. He seemed to know them all. When he reached the deck and started up the stairs, he found her eyes and stopped.

She nearly melted into a puddle but forced herself to play it cool. No way she was going to be like her mother— building a life around men who didn't bother to stick around in the morning. Pru had the highest of standards, and right now, she was all about starting over.

And her plan did not include romance.

"Surfer Girl," he said. He extended a hand in her direction. "I never caught your name."

She reached out and shook his hand, aware of a tingle that jumped down her spine as their skin touched. "I'm Prudence."

"Prudence," he said. "Meaning 'cautious.'"

She shrugged.

"Are you?" He was still holding her hand.

"Always."

That's when he flashed that smile. She was sure he'd been using that smile to get his way for a very long time by now. If her weak knees were any indication, he'd likely been very successful.

"I'm Hayes," he said. Finally, he released his grip on her hand and the coolness of the air signaled its absence. "Do you want to go for a walk?"

She regarded him for a long moment. "Did you hear me when I said I'm cautious?"

"Oh, right, and going for a walk on the beach with a stranger is probably the definition of reckless."

"Probably."

"What if we stay in full view of the party at all times?" he asked.

In retrospect, she probably should've said no. It wasn't smart to walk off with someone she didn't know. He could be a serial rapist. Or a murderer. Or a pervert.

Yet, something told her he was safe.

"Won't your adoring fans miss you?" she asked as he led her down the stairs and into the yard.

"I don't even know these people," he said.

"Hi, Hayes!" a girl's voice called out from the direction of the hot tub.

He waved, then turned back to Pru. He may be full of charisma, but she wasn't the only person who knew it— and that meant she was smarter to stick to her rules.

Just friends.

As they walked, Hayes pummeled her with questions. Where was she from? How'd she end up here? Was she going to college in the fall? Where'd she learn to surf like that?

And amazingly, he listened to all of her answers.

Originally a small town on the coast in Florida. She came

with a friend, then got a job at a surf shop. No money for college. She'd been told she was a natural talent on the board.

By the end of the night, Hayes knew more about her than anyone else. And not because she was intent on withholding information from others—but because he'd bothered to ask.

She returned the favor, and thanks to her line of questioning, she discovered that his family was not among the Nantucket wealthy but they spent summers there, that his parents made him work, and that his big dream was to travel the world.

"I like people," he'd told her. "I like finding out their stories."

"Clearly," she said. "You've asked me more questions tonight than the sum total of everyone else in my life."

She laughed to make sure he knew she wasn't sad about that, even though, in truth, she was.

Her own mother didn't know as much about her as this perfect stranger did now.

She dared a glance in his direction and found him watching her.

"You're a lot different than the other girls around here," he said.

She laughed, unsure if he meant it as a compliment but choosing to absolutely take it that way. "Thanks, I think?"

He nodded. "Definitely a compliment. You still won't let me take you out?"

She stopped walking and only then realized the party was no longer in view. "What if we just became really good friends?"

His lazy grin hitched for a split second, then came back brighter than before. "Friends."

"I'm not dating right now," she said. "But I could use a friend."

He held her gaze for *one-two-three*, then nodded once. "Friends it is."

And that's how it had been ever since.

Now, as the sun rose, there was a quiet knock on her door. She looked at the clock. Barely seven. What in the world?

She padded downstairs from the loft to the entryway, pulled the door open, and found Hayes standing outside. He wore that darn sexy navy blue peacoat, collar flipped up, a light scruff on his chin. The coat always made him look like a J. Crew model, and Pru had a hard time not daydreaming about his lips when he wore it.

He held up a to-go cup of coffee. "Did I wake you?"

She took the drink and stepped out of the way so he could come in, careful to secretly inhale the scent of him as he passed on by.

"Hayes, do you know what time it is?"

His eyes widened. "I shouldn't have come."

She laughed. "I wasn't asleep, it's fine."

"You either?"

She frowned. Would he ever tell her what it was that kept him up at night? "What are you doing here so early?"

"Just came to get a glimpse of you in your pajamas." He gave her a once-over and she instantly regretted the giant flannel Santa Claus pants and matching button-down pajama shirt she'd chosen before bed last night. "Cute, by the way."

She rolled her eyes and turned away, mostly to keep him from noticing she was blushing. "If you think I'm going to feed you again, you're crazy."

"Nah, I'm taking you to breakfast. I have a plan."

She frowned. "What kind of plan? And it's too early for food."

He shrugged the coat off and plopped down on the couch. "Sit."

She did as she was told, not because she was prone to obedience but because she was too tired to find a witty retort.

"Pru, I know this is going to sound crazy, but I felt it."

She took a sip of the hot coffee—peppermint mocha, her favorite. "Felt what?"

"The magic. It was like a zinger—no way I could ignore it."

Her heart sank. What was he talking about? Had he met someone? She must not have done a good job of hiding her concern because his smile faded into a frown.

"What's wrong?"

She took another drink, a silly attempt to hide at least a portion of her face. She shook her head. "Nothing. Did you meet someone?" Did that sound nonchalant?

His brow furrowed. "I'm talking about Peggy. The matchmaking."

Oh, thank God.

"Oh, right," she said.

He stared at her. "You okay?"

"Just tired." She rubbed her temples for effect, then slowly closed and opened her eyes.

"I can go?" He started to move. "Come back later?"

"It's fine," she said. "You're here, and now I need to hear about this magic."

He inched back on the couch and paused, as if for effect. "I found Peggy's match."

She lifted her brows to encourage him to continue, aware that his mouth had spread into a slow smile.

"Howie."

She set her cup down. "My Howie?"

"One and the same."

And then he launched into a crazy theory about Peggy having loved Howie a million years ago.

"I think he's the reason she never got married."

"You think Howie and . . . Peggy?"

"The magic says yes."

She almost laughed. "What's gotten into you? Yesterday you thought this was the dumbest thing ever."

He shrugged, then met her eyes, but only for a moment.

"What is it?"

"Nah, it's dumb."

"Hayes."

Another pause, then finally, he looked at her again. "She said we reminded her of them."

Pru went perfectly still. Her throat tightened. She managed to squeak out, "Really?"

He nodded. "Said she and whoever this guy was—they were inseparable. Like us. She also thought you and I were dating, by the way, but I set her straight."

Pru sat, unmoving, the air between them thick and tense. "Well, thank goodness."

He squinted at her. "You okay?"

"You asked me that already."

"And it still seems like you're not okay."

"I'm fine," she said, a little too quickly.

"Good, then what do we do about Peggy?" He was on

to the next topic while Pru was still basking in the beauty of his hazel eyes.

She forced herself to focus. She thought through the story he'd told her about Peggy and this mystery guy. "Well, you said she was in this guy's wedding, right? Whoever the love of her life was?"

Hayes took a drink and nodded. "She was the maid of honor."

"We can look up wedding announcements and see what we find," Pru said. "The library should have all the old newspapers, and weddings usually get full write-ups around here."

"See?" He grinned at her. "This is why I knew I had to break Aunt Nellie's rule and bring you in on this. I wouldn't have thought of that on my own."

She pushed a hand through her tangled dark waves and let her head fall back on the sofa. "I feel sorry for Peggy. She couldn't work up the courage to tell the man she loved how she felt and someone else swooped in and stole him from her."

"Let that be a lesson to you, Prudence Sutton," Hayes said with a flirtatious grin.

Pru sat up straighter and looked at him.

"One of these days, some beautiful woman is going to swoop in and steal me away."

She started to respond, but quickly snapped her jaw shut. What could she say? He was kidding—but it was true. She stayed silent about her real feelings because she didn't want to lose Hayes. But what did she think, that he was going to be there forever?

Some beautiful woman would surely appear, as if out of

thin air, steal his heart, and probably forbid him from ever seeing Prudence again. Because she, like everyone else in the world except for Hayes McGuire, would inevitably realize Pru wanted him to be so much more than her friend.

That this wasn't a little crush.

She was head over heels, completely in love with her best friend.

And that was the real plight of Prudence Sutton.

CHAPTER 10

A LOADED CONVERSATION

"*S*hould we head over to the library?" Hayes glanced at his watch. The Nantucket Atheneum probably wasn't even open yet. Why had he come over so early?

Because he couldn't sleep, that's why. And somehow, Pru's house put him at ease. Or maybe Pru put him at ease.

She settled back on the sofa and kicked her legs out from under her. "No need, we can look at the digital archives."

"Brilliant!" He should've thought of that. The Atheneum might've been a historic building, but it wasn't behind the times. With its solid white finish and grand stately columns, the building looked more like a monument than a library, and while Hayes didn't advertise this —once upon a time, it had been his escape.

He'd spent hours in the stacks, dreaming about faraway places. Now, he'd visited many of those places, wrote about distant, far-off lands, and thrived on discovering cultures that weren't his own.

Well, he *had* anyway. Somehow, since his last trip, that had changed. Now it almost seemed like the joy of exploring had been stolen from him. Just thinking of pitching a new story idea or traveling to a new place turned his insides. He hadn't updated his website in over a month. He knew he had to get over this.

He picked up Pru's feet and set them in his lap, settling into the opposite end of the couch the same way she had. "Should we look them up?"

"Mm-hmm." Pru nodded and closed her eyes—what had kept her up last night? She looked exhausted.

"My laptop is on the table next to you," she said.

He picked it up and navigated to the Atheneum's website, then found the digital directory chronicling newspaper articles that dated all the way back to the 1800s. He was accustomed to doing research for work, so he found his way around the website quickly and within minutes had located a write-up on the marriage of Howie Basford to Tamela Smith.

"Here it is," he said.

Pru's eyes opened. She had stunning blue eyes. It was a rare combination—dark hair and blue eyes—but then, she was a rare woman. After only a few days back in Nantucket, he couldn't deny there was something magnetic between them. True friends were like that though, weren't they? And while Hayes had never met a stranger, he didn't have a lot of close friends.

He wanted the very best for Pru, and he prayed she found it. But as soon as that thought popped in his head, something else twisted in his belly. He wanted Pru to be happy, of course, but the thought of her with a serious boyfriend—or worse, a husband—made him instantly jealous.

"And?" She sat up slightly but didn't pull her feet from his lap.

He quickly shook the thought away, forcing himself back to the matter at hand. "And I was right. The maid of honor, Peggy Swinton, wore a peach taffeta dress and matching shoes. She carried a small bouquet of white tulips."

Pru scrunched up her face. "Tammy never did have any taste."

Hayes laughed. "So, that settles it. Peggy was in love with Howie." He closed the laptop and set it aside, then thoughtlessly massaged Pru's feet. She wore red-and-white-striped fuzzy socks that matched her turquoise and red Santa pajamas, and she looked adorable.

Good grief. What was wrong with him? This was Prudence. Off-limits-to-him Prudence. Friends-and-nothing-more Prudence. Way-too-good-for-him Prudence.

"Peggy was in love with Howie," she repeated, but with more disbelief in her voice.

After a moment, Hayes said, "What a weird couple."

Pru laughed. "But you said it yourself—there was magic."

He couldn't deny that. Whatever spell Aunt Nellie had cast over him when she gave him that box, it was obviously doing its job. He'd even begun to think of his own love life—or the lack of one. But those thoughts were fleeting. He knew he was no good for another person right now, not when he had so many issues to work through.

The early morning sun shone through the windows of Pru's little cottage, bathing the entire space in a golden hue.

Hayes settled into the sofa, still holding her feet. Moments later, he noticed Pru's rhythmic breathing as her chest rose and fell in a long, drawn-out pattern. She'd fallen asleep. He took a moment to admire her smooth skin, and that buzzing feeling that seemed to accompany him daily ever since his trip home from his last assignment in the war-torn Middle East, began to settle.

He purposely set his breathing in time with hers, concentrating on the rise and fall of his own chest, thinking about how safe he felt, how peaceful, and then everything turned to black.

PRU AWOKE to the sun in her face and it took a moment to get her bearings. She felt groggy and out of sorts, and where was she?

She looked around and discovered she was on the couch in the middle of the living room, and Hayes was asleep on the other end. She glanced at the clock on the wall, piecing together the events of that morning—her long, sleepless night, Hayes knocking on her door before dawn, the coffee, looking up Howie's wedding announcement, realizing Hayes was right about her old friend and Peggy Swinton.

She found the clock on the wall. Eleven o'clock. Wow, she hadn't slept in that late in ages. Hayes slept soundly on her couch, holding on to her feet like a boy with a teddy bear. She'd been somewhat aware of him rubbing them, but she'd gotten so relaxed, it must've put her right to sleep. And now, she was waking up with Hayes.

Okay, not really, but she let herself cling to the fleeting thought, just for a minute.

She shifted slightly, and his eyes fluttered open. He looked around, confusion on his face. "I fell asleep."

"We both did." Pru pulled her legs from his lap and stood. "I guess we were tired."

He stretched. "I actually feel rested."

She glanced down at him. "Is that rare?"

He met her eyes, then looked away. "Unfortunately."

"You still don't want to talk about it?"

"Not really." He stood. "If that's okay."

"'Course." She picked up her half-empty coffee cup and walked toward the kitchen.

The house was bathed in sunlight and silence. Hayes followed her. "You need a Christmas tree."

She pulled a carton of eggs from the refrigerator and fetched a pan from the cupboard. "Eggs?"

"Sure." He pulled a loaf of bread out of a high cupboard and stuck four pieces in the toaster.

"I do need a Christmas tree," she said, cracking the eggs into a bowl. "I haven't had time." She stirred the eggs, then poured them in the pan.

"Let's go get one today," he said. "I'll help you decorate it."

She laughed. "Don't you have better things to do?" She found two plates and set them on the table while he made a fresh pot of coffee.

"Well, I came here for you, so not really."

The words lingered, threatening to give her away. *I came here for you.*

She righted herself with a nonchalant shrug. "All right, if that's how you want to spend your Sunday."

"Silverware?"

She moved out from in front of the drawer, and he opened it, grabbed the utensils, and finished setting the table.

"We can brainstorm ways to match Howie and Peggy."

"I'm not sure it's going to be an easy project," Pru said. "They're both set in their ways. What's Peggy going to do, retire and move to Hawaii or New Zealand or wherever Howie's living these days? She was born here; she's a Nantucketer."

Hayes cracked open a banana and took a bite. "Maybe she's ready for an adventure. Something new and exciting to spice up her third act."

Pru flipped the eggs as the toast popped, and Hayes buttered the warm bread. They moved in her small kitchen perfectly in sync, and she was keenly aware of it. She liked having him here—it put her at ease.

"Even if she is," Pru said, "you saw her—she's still hurt. Whatever happened between them, it was enough to stick with her for a long time."

They carried the food to the table and sat down. "I know what happened. Her best friend snagged him, and then Howie ditched her. She feels betrayed."

Pru grimaced. "And you're sure he's the one we're supposed to match her with?"

"Positive," Hayes said. "So, what would it take for her to realize she still has feelings for him?"

"Or what would it take for him to see her as more than

a friend?" The question was out before she could stop it. Her eyes darted to his and hung there like a lasso on the moon.

She looked away.

"Right," he said. "That would be tricky. If they had a history as friends, it would be hard to reimagine their relationship." He took a bite of toast and forced her gaze.

"True," she said cautiously. "But maybe he doesn't have those kinds of feelings for her. What if he wants to keep things as they are? Or were, I guess."

He washed down the bite with a sip of orange juice. "Then I guess she'll just have to do something to show him she's interested."

Pru frowned. "Why? Why can't it be on him to make the first move?"

"Well, she's a modern, independent woman," he said. "He wouldn't want to insult her by presuming she wasn't able to speak her mind."

Pru's heart raced. Why did this conversation feel loaded? They *were* talking about Howie and Peggy, right?

"And really," Hayes said, "what do they have to lose? You know, if they give it a try?"

Pru shifted. "A lot, actually."

He frowned. "Really?"

"I mean, she may really value the friendship. And what if it doesn't work out between them? She's just destroyed the best relationship in her life."

Hayes set his fork down and held her captive with those hazel eyes. "But they're not friends, Pru. They haven't spoken in years."

Well, shoot.

93

"Right," she said dumbly. "They're not friends. So, we need to maybe concentrate on getting them talking again."

"Right." He pushed a hand through his hair, which, it turned out, was an incredibly sexy thing to do. That simple action left it perfectly mussed.

"Uh . . . I'm going to go," he said. "I'll be back in a little while to go get your tree."

She pushed her plate of half-eaten food away from her, her appetite gone.

"I'll be back," he repeated.

"Okay," she said. "See ya in a little bit." Her mouth went dry.

What had she done? She'd let that conversation get away from her. She'd spooked him with her nonsensical talk.

And she had no idea how to take back what she'd said.

CHAPTER 11

HEART OTHERWISE ENGAGED

*H*ayes raced out of Pru's house, mind spinning, heart pounding.

One minute they were talking about Howie and Peggy and the next minute—well, he wasn't sure who they were talking about.

Pru's questions, along with that indescribable sense of calm he'd felt in her presence had his mind tumbling. Add that to the conversation they'd just had, and all Hayes could think about was running away.

What on earth was going on?

He hurried back to his parents' cottage, showered, got dressed, then sat on the edge of his bed, replaying the conversation over and over in his mind. Downstairs, he could hear his family, taking advantage of the long holiday weekend by playing a rousing game of gin at the kitchen table. They laughed and spoke loudly, and Hayes could've sat down with them and pretended to be as laid-back and easy-going as they all thought he was.

He could crack jokes and tell stories and keep them all

entertained. After all, that was his role. But somehow, he couldn't muster the energy.

This whole matchmaking thing was getting out of hand. He was supposed to be concentrating on Peggy, finding her perfect match—and instead, he couldn't stop thinking maybe it was time he got serious about his own.

And Pru happened to be occupying all of those thoughts. But she was off-limits, especially to him. Hayes wasn't a serious relationship kind of guy. And Pru was a *till death do us part* kind of girl.

He wasn't good enough for her, and he knew it. Besides, she didn't think of him that way—she'd made that clear how many times over the years?

He opened the box Aunt Nellie had left him and pulled everything out. Maybe there was some secret Noni Rose magic inside that he hadn't uncovered. Something to keep him from getting too wrapped up in it, to stay focused on the task at hand.

He flipped open Nellie's small scrapbook and read through the success stories, carefully detailed by the matchmakers who'd made them happen. Maybe it would spark an idea about Peggy and Howie—that was the relationship he should be focusing on, after all.

He moved on to a manila envelope that had been neatly tucked in the bottom of the box. Inside, he found a stack of loose papers. On the top was a sticky note that read "Unsuccessful Matches."

Aunt Nellie hadn't mentioned any unsuccessful attempts. Maybe there wasn't some great pressure to get this right. Maybe Peggy would be just fine if Hayes failed and she ended up alone.

And yet, that didn't seem right either. While he didn't

consider himself a romantic, he'd certainly noticed that zap between Peggy and Howie. It was undeniable, really. Even after all this time, the spark was still there. He had to at least try to get them together.

He shuffled the papers, each detailing a Nantucket native who hadn't been matched. Reasons were written at the bottom.

Left the island.

Too focused on career to settle down.

Heart otherwise engaged.

He stopped. He was staring at a photo of Pru. His eyes went back to the bottom of the page, where someone (Aunt Nellie?) had written *Heart otherwise engaged.*

What?

There was no date on the sheet, but maybe Pru had been holding out on him. Maybe she'd fallen for someone and never told him. His heart wrenched. Why? He would be happy for her if she found someone who made her happy. Of course he would.

So why the sick feeling in his stomach?

Hayes folded the paper and stuck it in his pocket. He'd head straight over and make her tell him the truth. Weren't they supposed to be best friends? He thought for sure when she fell in love, he'd be the first to know.

They used to joke that he'd be her maid of honor—after all, he *was* her best friend.

Heart otherwise engaged.

The words raced through his head, and a deep sense of loss wound its way through him. But no, Pru wasn't in love—if she was, surely, she would be in a relationship. No guy in his right mind would turn her down. But it had been a long time since he and Pru had occupied the same space. Just because she didn't talk about dating anyone didn't mean she hadn't. And if she had, maybe she'd fallen —hard.

Maybe she was too embarrassed or too hurt to talk about it.

His stomach—the little traitor—turned yet again at the thought.

So far, his plan to stay focused on matchmaking Peggy and Howie had gone awry. He didn't like this side of himself, but Pru was his to protect. If someone had hurt her, he needed to know about it. She didn't have anyone else.

He reached her house, hurried up the walk, and knocked on the door, ready to ask her why her heart was otherwise engaged.

But when she opened it, standing there in her red stocking cap and matching red scarf, the question disappeared.

He didn't want to know the answer. He didn't want to believe that Pru had fallen in love with someone. It was selfish, and he knew it—he didn't begrudge her happiness.

But Pru was *his.*

"You okay?" she asked. "You look weird."

"I'm great," he said, a little too cheerily. "Let's go get a Christmas tree."

She smiled up at him and his breath caught in his throat. What a fool he'd been. He didn't want them to turn into Howie and Peggy. He wanted Pru.

She frowned. "You ready?"

He nodded. "Yeah, of course. Let's go." He swallowed his thoughts because he knew deep down that changing his relationship with Pru was a huge deal. And besides, it would take both of them to do that, and Pru didn't think very highly of him when it came to his past relationships. Never mind that her thoughts weren't exactly backed up by fact. He didn't have a string of women all over the world or anything like that, but he did keep every relationship casual, and Pru had zero respect for that.

He wasn't good for her. Not good enough anyway. Especially not right now, when he felt so lost, when he still had so much to sort out.

He kept his thoughts to himself as they walked around Moors End Farm, shopping for the perfect Christmas tree —not too tall, but plenty full.

Pru stopped in front of a tree and grinned. "This is it."

He gave it a once-over and nodded. "Good choice."

They paid for it, then loaded it on top of Pru's SUV and drove back to her house. When they arrived, he dragged it inside and set it up while she located a small box of mostly handmade Christmas ornaments.

She turned on Christmas music while they decorated, and not for one second did he find any of it cheesy. In fact, he considered it to be a near-perfect way to pass the time. Best of all, the angst he'd felt earlier had mostly disappeared.

She made hot cocoa and when they were finished with the tree, she floated the idea of baking Christmas cookies. Of course, he agreed. Neither of them mentioned Peggy or Howie. Aunt Nellie might not approve, but he simply didn't want to think about anyone but Prudence.

The day faded into night, and they settled back on the couch for a viewing of *It's a Wonderful Life*, and once again, Hayes was overcome with comfort.

Pru felt like home.

The note from Aunt Nellie's box was tucked inside the pocket of his peacoat, but he couldn't bring himself to ask Pru about it. Why, he wasn't sure. Pru was his friend. And yet, the thought of her being in love with someone—someone who wasn't him . . .

"I love this part," Pru said, staring at the screen. There was a big bowl of popcorn between them, and the flickering blue light of the television painted her in a faint, hazy glow.

"Pru, I found something today," he said without thinking. Truth be told, he hadn't been paying much attention to the movie.

She looked at him. "Did you hear me when I said I love this part?" She smiled.

He didn't. He'd turned serious, and there was no going back.

She paused the movie. "What did you find? Something else about Howie and Peggy?"

He leaned over to grab his coat from the back of the armchair he'd flung it over and pulled the page from his pocket. *No turning back now.*

When she looked at it, her eyes widened. "What is this?"

"It was in the matchmaker box."

She scanned the page, eyes inevitably landing on the phrase *Heart otherwise engaged.* "I don't understand."

"I guess Noni Rose tried to match you," he said.

If she was angry about this, Pru didn't let on.

"You never mentioned anything to me about seriously dating anyone," he said.

She folded the paper and handed it back to him.

"Because I didn't seriously date anyone." She pulled her legs up underneath her.

"Oh." He studied her. Was she in love with someone she shouldn't be? Someone married? "You don't have to tell me. I was just wondering."

She turned toward him. "I don't know what Aunt Nellie thought she knew, but my heart is as unattached as it's always been."

"Oh," he said. "Okay."

But something told him she wasn't being honest. She was holding back.

He thought of the several times she'd asked him why he wasn't sleeping. He was holding back too, and he didn't want to anymore. Not here, not with Pru.

The white light from the Christmas tree glowed behind them, and the coziness of the fire enveloped them in peaceful comfort.

"I saw someone die," he said now, certain talking about this wasn't going to end well.

Pru stilled.

He hadn't told anyone what had happened on his trip through the Middle East. In retrospect, he probably shouldn't have gone. He'd been doing a series on finding beauty in unlikely places, and it had been very well received—it turned out a lot of people want to travel to countries that aren't known for being tourist destinations.

In hindsight, he'd been foolish and arrogant to think he could leave there unscathed.

But if there was anyone in the world who would listen without judging him, it was Pru.

And he wanted her to know.

So he told her the whole story. He told her how he

went to Egypt, against the better judgment of everyone in his professional circle. How he was walking through the market, minding his own business, when across the street, a man got into a car and started the engine.

"I can still see his face," Hayes said. "He was young, maybe early twenties. I don't know what he was mixed up in or if he was one of the good guys, but he turned the ignition and there was this horrible sound—an explosion, then screams throughout the street."

Hayes felt the blast of the car bomb from where he stood. It heated his face. In the commotion, someone pushed him down, but he couldn't get the man's face out of his head. Hayes had watched him walk out of a nearby restaurant. They'd made eye contact before the man got in his car.

And now he was dead. Just like that.

He spilled the entire story, surprising even himself, and now sat, mesmerized by the twinkling white lights they'd strung on the mantel behind Pru.

She didn't say anything. She simply moved closer and held him, perfectly still, as the sadness oozed out of him. He didn't like to be that guy—the one with issues. He was Hayes McGuire, life of the party. But not with Pru. With Pru, he could be whoever he was and feel whatever he felt.

He was tired of pretending, and she was his safe place.

They sat for a long time, and Hayes tried not to relive the horror over and over again. The fire flickered and Jimmy Stewart's still face stared at them from the paused movie on the television screen.

It was quiet and peaceful, and Pru smelled so good, like cookies and cinnamon. He wrapped his arms around her and lay back, her body nestled between him and the back of the couch, her head on his chest. This wasn't weird, right? They were friends. This was perfectly normal.

He'd stopped thinking about Pru as anything else when she turned him down—twice—confident he could be the friend she needed. That didn't stop just because they were practically cuddling on her sofa.

She clicked the movie on and they watched till the end, but as the credits rolled, he

discovered she'd fallen asleep on him.

Heart otherwise engaged.

He knew why he didn't want that to be true. He knew it, but he'd never admit it out loud because admitting it meant that his feelings for Pru had changed, and he couldn't let that happen—not if he wanted to keep her in his life. But as he drifted off to sleep, he tried not to think about waking her up and kissing her. It wasn't easy, he was overcome with the desire.

He needed his head and heart to get in line.

But it'd be a whole lot easier if her body wasn't tucked in his arms.

CHAPTER 12

THE MORNING AFTER

*M*orning sun filtered in through the windows, turning the living room bright white. Pru squinted as her eyes opened and she discovered she was on the couch again, this time using Hayes as her pillow.

Had she slept here? On the couch? With Hayes?

She lifted her head ever so slightly.

And *oh my gosh*—had she drooled on Hayes's shirt?

She swiped at her cheek and backed away to discover that she had, in fact, drooled on the man. But she also realized she'd slept soundly through the night. Maybe he wouldn't notice. His head was tilted slightly away from her, but his lips were *right there*. If she wanted, she could wake him with kisses.

What would it be like to have the right to do that?

She put a hand on his chest, marveling at the rise and fall of his breathing, and still processing the things he'd told her the night before. No wonder the spark in his eyes had gone. No wonder he always looked tired.

In just a few days, they'd attend the preview party, then the stroll and then, as far as she knew, he would board the ferry and go, off to live a life that, for the most part, didn't include Pru.

Slowly, she slid from his grasp, thankful she didn't wake him. She brushed her teeth and finger-combed her hair, then stood outside the bathroom staring at Hayes, fast asleep on her sofa.

He'd rolled over onto his side but still breathed deeply, and it was a wonder to watch him like that—beautiful and peaceful and . . . beautiful. She could've told him last night how she felt about him. She could've said she didn't want to end up like Peggy, sitting with the weight of regret, having never spoken up about her real feelings.

But in the end, she'd chosen silence, just like always. Because she couldn't lose Hayes. She loved him too much to ever even consider that he wouldn't be a part of her life.

She couldn't stand that thought. She'd resigned herself to taking him however she could get him.

She pulled on her boots and coat, then rushed off down the street to pick up coffee and pastries, but when she returned to her cottage, she found it empty.

Hayes had left a note on her kitchen table.

Had to go help Mom with some stuff at home. Thanks for listening last night. You're the best! –Hayes

She stared at the words until they lost their meaning. She texted him:

You left before coffee.

Sorry. And thanks for last night.
Anytime.

She stared at the phone as the three magical dots appeared, then disappeared. She waited a minute before deciding the conversation was over. She looked at the freshly decorated Christmas tree. On the top, instead of an angel or a star, Hayes had affixed a photo of the two of them that he'd printed from his phone the night before.

The truth was, she'd let herself daydream last night. Enough to make herself blush as she thought about it now. She'd pretended they were a couple from the moment they set out looking for a tree, and she'd carried on with the mental charade until she woke up in his arms that morning.

This was probably unhealthy.

She didn't want to wonder if she and Hayes might actually be soulmates. But she also didn't want to lose him.

She opened the white wax-paper bag from the coffee shop, pulled out the blueberry scone, and took a bite. The way she felt, she'd probably also eat the bear claw intended for Hayes.

Heart otherwise engaged.

Was it ever. Aunt Nellie knew it. Howie knew it. And maybe it was time Hayes knew it too.

But Pru had a feeling she wasn't that brave.

HAYES TEXTED Pru the next day:

I have an idea. Can you get Howie to the Ale House for dinner tomorrow night?

Sure, I can ask.

K. 7 p.m. Boiler Room. You meet me there at 6:30.

You got it, Noni Rose. ;)

Funny. I'm never gonna live this down, am I?

Not a chance.

CHAPTER 13

A FOOLPROOF PLAN

*P*ru arrived at the Ale House promptly at 6:30 p.m. Wednesday night and found Hayes waiting for her in the entryway.

"Is Howie coming?"

"His calendar is shockingly open," she said. "Or maybe he just cleared it for me." She followed Hayes through the restaurant to a room near the back, usually reserved for private parties. It had been decorated for the holidays and, like the rest of the space, dazzled under the shine of hundreds of twinkling white lights.

On Nantucket, everything twinkled and glowed at Christmas.

At the center of the room were two tables, each decorated with a sprig of evergreen in a vase tied with a red plaid ribbon.

"I can't believe this room is open," she said. "It's the holiday season."

"The owner is a friend. He shuffled a few things around."

"We didn't ruin someone else's night, did we?" she asked.

"Of course not," he said. "You're always so concerned about everyone else."

She frowned. "And that's bad?"

He found her eyes and shook her head. "Just one more thing to admire about you."

She felt her breath hitch, and she forced herself to recover. "So what's the plan, we wait for them, then all have dinner together?"

"No," he said with a smile. "We never show."

She frowned. "We can't do that."

"Why not? It's perfect. They'll sit here in silence for a few minutes, and we text them to tell them we're running late, but to go ahead and start without us, and before you know it, they'll be having dinner together."

She eyed him for a long moment. "How'd you get Peggy to agree to this anyway?"

"Are you kidding?" He smiled. "Do you think I have trouble getting women to go to dinner with me?"

"You're the weirdest matchmaker I've ever met in my life." She shook her head. "And the least subtle."

"Aunt Nellie said nothing about subtle," he said.

"Well, they aren't supposed to know they're being matched," Pru told him. "This is so obvious."

"But by the end of the night, they'll be so in love with each other it won't matter."

"You're awfully confident." She crossed her arms over her chest and shook her head.

"My buddy also set us up in the office so we can watch on the security camera."

She gasped. "That's a huge violation of privacy."

He looked her over. "Tell me you're not dying to see how this plays out."

Well, shoot. She was, actually.

"There's no sound, so it's not *exactly* an ethical violation," Hayes said. "Follow me."

He led her through the kitchen, which was noisy and loud and bustling with activity, and into an office off to the side. On the desk were three small screens, each showing different parts of the restaurant. Periodically, the images changed.

"Is your friend paranoid?" Pru asked.

"Just cautious," a voice from behind her said.

She turned and saw a hulking man in a chef's uniform. He extended a beefy hand in Hayes's direction and grinned. "Good to see you, my friend."

"Thank you for doing this, Dante," Hayes said. "This is Pru."

"Sutton Surf," he said. "I've been in your shop."

"Good to meet you." Pru smiled, and noticed the wedding ring on Dante's left hand. On the desk was a photo of his family—a wife and two kids. Pru wouldn't deny she longed for a family of her own. Being hung up on Hayes was keeping her from finding that, and she knew it. If she wanted to have kids, she probably shouldn't be wasting time on a fantasy that was never going to happen.

Inwardly, she groaned. She hated the universe's little reminders that she wasn't getting any younger.

Dante glanced at Hayes and raised his eyebrows. Silent communication passed between the two men. It was fleeting, and Pru didn't dare ask what it was about—the last thing she needed was a picture into the inner workings of a man's mind.

Although, knowing what Hayes was thinking could come in handy sometimes.

"Order whatever you want." Dante produced two menus. "On me."

"You really don't have to do that," Pru said.

"Yes, he does." Hayes grinned. "He owes me."

"He's right," Dante said. "I'd do anything for this guy. I'll be back in a few to get your orders."

Hayes studied the menu a bit too intently.

"Why does he owe you?" Pru asked.

Hayes shrugged. "I was the seed money in this place."

Pru set her menu down. "You own part of this restaurant?"

"Why is that so surprising?" Hayes didn't look up from the menu.

"I didn't realize you were doing so well," she said.

He smirked. "Well, when my dad started investing, he taught us everything he learned. I've been growing my portfolio ever since I worked at the Yacht Club when I was sixteen."

"So, you're rich?"

"No, but I do okay," he said. "Dante's a friend, and a killer chef. Wait till you taste his food. He didn't have a way to open a place of his own, and I saw an opportunity."

"Don't pretend you did this to make money, Hayes," she said, looking over the menu. "You did it to make that guy's dreams come true. Same way you sent all those surfers my way the first summer after Howie sold me the shop. I think I had fifteen orders for custom boards in two weeks' time."

He smiled. "What can I say? I'm a helper."

"Maybe Aunt Nellie *did* know what she was doing," Pru said.

Dante returned and took their orders, and then they settled in to two chairs at the desk. It was the first time she'd ever eaten a high-end dinner at a desk, watching surveillance footage.

Howie arrived first. The hostess brought him to the room and sat him at one of the two tables, then vanished. A few minutes later, Peggy arrived and was seated at the second table.

Hayes took off his suitcoat. "Now we're talking." He rubbed his hands together like things were about to get good.

"You know this could all backfire, right?" Pru asked.

"What kind of talk is that?" he said with faux shock. "This is a foolproof plan."

Dante brought two beautiful plates and set them on the desk in front of them, then looked at the screen. "This is the couple we're working on?"

"Yep," Hayes said. "We have a hunch they belong together."

The chef looked at Pru, then back at Hayes. "Uh-huh. Let me know if you need anything else." He closed the door behind him as he left, shutting them in the small, dark office. A pine wreath hung on the wall, along with handmade cards that read *I love you, Daddy* and a photo of Dante and his wife.

Hayes pulled out his phone and texted Peggy, talking aloud as he did. "Running late. Should be there in about ten minutes."

They watched as Peggy pulled her phone from her purse, read the text, then set it down on the table.

So far, Peggy and Howie didn't seem to be speaking. They were each sitting at their own table, staring off in the opposite direction of the other person. Howie didn't seem the shy type, but maybe he'd been awful to Peggy and he didn't know how to make it up to her.

"It feels tense," Pru said, eating a bite of her spaghetti and meatballs. The flavors of garlic and tomato burst in her mouth. "Oh my gosh, this is the best thing I've ever tasted."

Hayes smiled. "I told you. He does this chicken marsala that's to die for. And his steak—here, taste it." He cut a piece of his filet, ran it through the juices pooling at the edge of the plate, and fed it to her from his fork.

She nodded as she chewed, affirming his opinion on Dante's capabilities. "Good investment."

He grinned, then scooped a bite of mashed potatoes into his mouth. "Told ya. Now you think I'm a genius."

"Let's not get crazy."

On cue, the hostess arrived with a platter of appetizers for Howie. She'd been instructed to tell him that Pru was on her way, and to enjoy a bite while he waited. Now, they were counting on the man's good manners. Surely, he wouldn't let Peggy sit there by herself while he ate in front of her.

They watched for a long minute, and nothing happened. Maybe Howie *would* eat the appetizers in front of her.

"Is he really that rude?" Pru asked, exasperated. "Come on, dude!"

"Maybe he asked, and she declined." It wasn't like they

could make out exactly what was happening—the video was fuzzy at best.

"How hard would it be?" Pru said, then, affecting Howie's laid-back California-surfer accent, she added, "Peggy, would you like to share in this platter of appetizers that magically appeared on my table?"

"Well, sure, I thought you'd never ask," Hayes said, raising his voice in an attempt to sound more feminine.

Pru frowned. "Why did you give her a Southern accent?"

Hayes grimaced. "I was going for girly."

"Try again."

He repeated the sentence, this time with less of a drawl, and Pru considered it decent enough to continue.

"And while we're talking, I wanted to let you know how sorry I am that I didn't notice you standing right in front of me all those years," Pru continued. "Maybe I took you for granted."

"No, Howie, I understand," Hayes said, still using that voice. "I should've spoken up and told you how I felt."

"Don't sweat it, Peg," Pru said, still doing her best Howie impression. "I know how hard it can be to speak your mind when there's so much on the line. Maybe I should've made the first move."

"Oh, don't be too hard on yourself. I know how difficult it can be to take that step, and by the time you realized you were in love with me, our friendship was far too important to risk it," Hayes said.

"Exactly right," Pru said, dropping the voice. She turned toward Hayes and found him watching her. She stuttered. "I—I mean, I'm sure that's what they're saying."

Hayes's expression turned serious as he met her eyes. "Do you think?"

Pru's stomach wobbled as she nodded. "If they were good friends, it would've been such a big risk."

"But it might've been worth it."

She went still, the air between them thick. "But how do they know if it is?"

They sat now, only inches apart, neither of them eating, staring at each other as if they were carved in stone.

"What are we doing here, Pru?" Hayes asked.

She shifted but maintained eye contact. She didn't want to run away from her feelings anymore. The risk was worth it—wasn't it? If she never put herself out there, she'd always wonder. And yet, she still played dumb with Hayes. "What do you mean?"

"You and me." Hayes pushed a hand through his hair, and a look of desperation skittered across his face. "What is this?"

"We're friends," she said.

He scooted closer, eyes intent on her. "I don't want to end up like them."

Her breath caught. Her throat tightened. Her stomach somersaulted. What was he saying? His gaze remained steady—intent on her.

"Hayes, I—"

But he didn't let her finish. His hands framed her face and he closed the gap between them, letting his lips softly graze hers, so gentle they seemed to ask for permission. Her mind spun. There was no going back now, so she might as well enjoy it—she kissed him back, and not gently, but the way she'd been dreaming of doing for years now. She gave herself over with such complete and reckless abandon, her stomach somersaulted again, and she completely forgot they were sitting in Dante's office.

She drank him in as his hands wound around her back, pulling her body to his, her hands tangled in his hair, lost in each other as if they were the only two people in the world at that moment.

When he finally pulled away from her, she was breathless and stupid with desire.

But in a flash, Hayes's expression turned worried—brow furrowed, mouth slightly agape.

Pru's heart plummeted into her belly. *Was it a mistake? Does he regret it?*

"Pru—I'm sorry—we—"

But before he could finish, she glanced at the screen and saw that Peggy had stood up. Hayes's phone dinged a new text.

"She's leaving," Pru said.

Hayes read the text and nodded. "Yep, she is. She said she had to go, but we could reschedule."

Pru stood. "We have to stop her."

Hayes glanced back to the screen, where Howie still sat, looking fuzzy and forlorn. "Maybe too much interference is a bad thing."

She watched as Peggy moved out of the frame. "You're just going to let her walk away?"

He sighed, seemingly indifferent. "Maybe it's too late for them. Maybe we were fooling ourselves to think they were supposed to be more than friends."

She took a step back. "Hayes, what are you saying?"

He turned, like a rat in a cage. "You're my best friend,

Prudence. And I just screwed everything up. Nothing will be the same now."

Pru searched for a reply but came up empty. "I'm going to go find Peggy."

She darted out before he could stop her and before he could see the tears streaming down her face.

At least she had her answer. She and Hayes were never supposed to be more than just friends.

And now, thanks to a moment of weakness, they may not even be that.

CHAPTER 14

LIKE A CHICKEN

*H*ayes watched her leave. He didn't go after her like he should've. He just stood there, like an idiot, regretting and not regretting his impulsive decision to kiss her like she was oxygen and he was underwater.

What was he thinking? It was Pru.

The truth was, that kiss had terrified him. The feelings it mined inside of him were fierce and unwavering, like a dam had burst and the rush of water took over. He'd never felt this kind of pull to another person—not even Kara, and for a long time he'd thought he'd loved her.

He knew better now. What he'd felt for his college girlfriend was simply infatuation. Nothing like what he was feeling now, and even still, that breakup had been brutal—could he possibly be ready to try again?

No, Hayes didn't do relationships, not the kind Pru deserved. Once they went down this path, that was it. *For as long as we both shall live.*

He wasn't ready. They weren't ready. And it would be a miracle if she ever talked to him again.

He whipped out his phone and sent her a text:

I'M SO SORRY, *Pru. We need to talk.*

HE WAITED to the count of ten before clicking his phone off. She wasn't responding. Could he blame her? She was either freaked out by his mixed messages or as horrified as he was that they'd just crossed that invisible, unspoken, always-present line.

What was he thinking?

But man, that was some kiss. It made him curious and excited and anxious to do it again. He didn't think he could go on being "just friends" with Pru. Could he be the man she deserved?

He glanced at the screen and saw that Howie was still sitting there, alone.

He hesitated to leave the perfectly cooked, half-eaten filet mignon on the desk, but he didn't want to miss a chance to talk to the man—find out what had really happened between him and Peggy.

He raced out of the office and into the private room, where he found Howie nursing a beer and staring out the window toward the street.

"You just missed her." Howie took a swig.

Hayes didn't bother to tell him he knew he'd missed her—he'd been watching like a creeper on a video camera in the back room.

"Mind if I sit?"

Howie motioned to the chair opposite him, then regarded Hayes for a long moment. He sighed. "Can I give you a bit of advice?"

Hayes leaned back in his chair. "Sure."

"Don't be an idiot."

Hayes frowned. "You think I'm an idiot?"

Howie laughed. "Well, maybe, but I was talking about myself."

"How so?"

"Did you know Peggy and I used to be good friends?" Howie asked. "Best friends, actually."

"Like me and Pru."

Howie's gave him a knowing look. "Yeah, like that."

"I admit I do know a little bit about your history," Hayes said.

Howie glanced down at the tray of appetizers on his table. "Hungry?"

Hayes was, in fact. His mind wandered back to the steak he'd left behind, and his mouth practically watered for it. Howie set a small plate in front of him. "Go ahead. Pru isn't coming. She had them send this out to tide me over, but then she texted and said something came up."

A flash of the scene that had just played out in the office raced through his mind. He liked kissing her—more than liked it, really—why was he fighting it? What if they could be great together?

Or what if he ended up hurting her because he couldn't be what she needed? He did have a way of botching relationships.

Hayes picked up two stuffed mushrooms and put them on his plate. "I'm starving, actually."

"Dig in," Howie said.

They ate in silence for a few minutes, then Howie took

a sip of water and folded his hands on the table. "What do you know? About me and Peg?"

"That you were an idiot." Hayes grinned.

"If I'm honest, I always loved Peggy," Howie said. "Thought she didn't look at me as anything other than a friend. Like a brother, actually. We had a pretty unique relationship."

Hayes understood.

"She was quiet, and I was scared. Peggy was the real deal, you know? Someone you make a commitment to." He stilled. "Like Pru."

Hayes's eyes darted to Howie's, but he didn't respond.

"Why didn't you do anything about it back then?" Hayes asked, looking for insight into his own romantic quandary. "What kept you from taking the risk?"

Howie looked at him. "She was the most important person in the world to me, kid. But Peggy and I are very different. Believe it or not, she was the one who wanted to travel and see the world. I was hooked on Nantucket. I never in a million years thought we'd trade places."

"But she loves it here," Hayes said. "She's practically the town historian. And adventure doesn't really seem like her thing.

"Yeah, but, she had a different side to her back then. Peggy was always going to see the world. She had her passport and her big dream was to get as many stamps as she could."

"Wow," Hayes said. "What changed?"

"Her mom got sick, and she had to stay and take care of her. I think between that and, well, me—her spirit got crushed." Howie's face fell. "I guess she settled for safe after that."

Nothing good ever came from playing it safe, did it?

"So, if you had it to do over . . . ?" Hayes asked.

"No question," Howie said. "I would've wised up sooner and told her the truth—" He shrugged. "And maybe it would've crashed and burned. Maybe she would've turned me down. Flown off to Nigeria to build orphanages or something. Or maybe she would've loved me back. But the regret I've been living with—it's so much worse than never knowing what could've been."

Hayes chewed on that for a long moment before responding. "So, what now? Did you talk to her tonight?"

"Sadly, I think I waited too long, and I hurt her. I'm not sure she's ever gonna be ready to let me back in her life. I'm afraid we missed our chance." Howie sighed. "But you haven't."

Howie might talk like an old surfer, but he wasn't an idiot. Hayes looked away.

"Come on, young buck," Howie said. "I can see it all over your face—you're a very conflicted man."

"I wasn't—until tonight." Hayes's mind still spun with thoughts of that kiss. He wasn't sure what had come over him. He didn't usually think of Pru that way—she'd placed him strictly in the friend zone, and he'd respected that for a long time. But in recent days—everything had changed. When the rest of the world made no sense, she did.

"Don't make the same mistake I made," Howie said. "Don't wait."

Hayes looked at him. If anyone understood what he was going through, it was Howie. He hadn't followed his heart and look where it landed him—a world away from the woman he could've been loving his entire life. It was like life had laid out its very own cautionary tale right there in front of him. It didn't take a genius to see it.

"Pru and I are—"

"Best friends," Howie interrupted. "I know. Peggy was my best friend too, once upon a time."

Hayes paused for a beat. "I should go. Order dinner. On me."

"Nah, I think I'll head out too."

Hayes wasn't a great comforter, that had always been Pru's role. But now, looking at Howie, he could practically see the sadness radiating off of him.

"Maybe it's not too late," Hayes said. "Maybe she just needs to see that you're willing to fight for her. Or that you regret it? I mean, if she's worth it, you shouldn't give up so easily, right?"

Howie emptied his bottle and set it down on the table. "You really think so?"

Hayes shrugged. "What've you got to lose?"

He waved a hand in the air. "I wouldn't know where to start. I'm an old guy now, and I have no idea how to start dating again."

"I'm sure you've still got some tricks up your sleeve," Hayes said with a laugh. "Why don't you start with an apology? Some flowers? A little bit of groveling? Women like to be wooed."

Howie's jaw twitched, and he appeared to be considering his options.

Hayes could see—feel—the older man's insecurity. Didn't that ever go away? But he understood—putting your heart on the line was no easy task no matter how old you were. "You know, you'll both be at the preview party on Thursday. I've got an idea."

"Yeah?"

"Just be ready, okay?" Hayes stood. "I've got a plan. But send flowers anyway—and don't be cheap about it." He'd started out the door when Howie stopped him. He turned back and found the older man still sitting at the table, looking slightly pathetic.

"I meant what I said, kid," he admonished. "Don't wait. She's worth the risk."

The words hung there—a warning if he'd ever heard one—and finally, after several seconds, Hayes nodded, then walked away, replaying the highlights of the conversation in his mind.

That kiss still had his head spinning in circles—he wasn't thinking clearly. Or maybe, for the first time, he was. Maybe Pru was right, and there really was one person for everyone. And Pru was that person for him. It's why every other relationship he attempted felt so empty. Because he compared every other woman to her.

And none of them even came close.

He skipped the car in favor of a walk—the fresh, crisp air would do him good—and his path was illuminated by the dozens of lit Christmas trees lining the street. He turned a corner and strode toward her house, a place of comfort and peace—not because of the four walls, but because of who was inside.

She'd calmed the anxiety inside him, and he'd been carrying it around with him for months. Pru had captivated him the moment he saw her emerge from the waves all those years ago.

He had to tell her. He didn't want to end up like Howie.

Down the block, he saw her pull up in front of her

house and park her SUV on the street. The headlights turned off, and she got out. He stood back—watching her like a crazy stalker—or like a man who'd had a revelation.

He loved her. He'd loved kissing her. He wanted to do it again and for a very long time.

A niggle of a reminder played at the back of his mind. He knew he wasn't good enough for Pru. He knew that she wasn't the kind of woman he could just casually date. He knew if he took this step, it would likely lead to another trip—straight down the aisle.

Was he really ready for that? Was he really the kind of guy who could commit to that? How would she handle his vagabond lifestyle? Or would being with her mean he had to give that up?

He watched as she opened the door to her house and went inside.

There was a lot more to this than a simple proclamation of love. He had to be sure. This was too important to get wrong. She was too important to lose.

Maybe they both needed to sleep on it. Because if he was going to lose her, he didn't want to do it tonight.

So, like a chicken, Hayes went back to the restaurant, got in the McGuire family island car, and drove home, where he spent a very long, very sleepless night. And it had nothing to do with what he'd seen in the Middle East.

PRU HAD SEEN the regret on Hayes's face the second he pulled from her arms. It was a look she'd been dreading, a look she'd never forget.

His words echoed at the back of her mind—he said

he'd screwed everything up. Obviously, he regretted that kiss.

Never mind that she could still taste him on her lips. Never mind she loved that she could.

She'd run out onto the street and found Peggy walking gingerly on the icy sidewalk. She linked arms with the woman, practically a stranger, and they walked all the way to Peggy's house, barely talking. It was almost as if a quiet understanding existed in their silence.

Now, in the quiet comfort of her little cottage, she checked her phone and saw that Hayes had texted.

I'm so sorry, Pru. We need to talk.

But she wouldn't text him back tonight. Tomorrow, she knew she'd have to pretend the kiss meant nothing. That she agreed with him it was a mistake. But tonight, she wanted to imagine—even for a little while—that the Nantucket Christmas magic might've actually been at work on her behalf.

Tonight, she'd fall asleep dreaming that the kiss had changed everything between them, the way she'd been hoping of for a whole lot longer than she cared to admit.

CHAPTER 15

A ROOF WITH A VIEW

"You've been avoiding me." Hayes's voice turned her around. She was standing in the entryway of the Nantucket Whaling Museum, waiting for him to escort her into the preview party. She'd told him not to pick her up at her house because this way it seemed less like a date. This way, her fantasies might stay rooted in realism. This way, she might be able to go forward with her plan to let him off the hook for what had happened in the office the night before.

She *had* been avoiding him. She'd left her house early that morning and hadn't returned until late. She'd gone to the surf shop to work on one of the custom boards she needed to get finished, and took far too long sanding and glassing it because she was so distracted.

Typically, working on a board calmed her nerves, but not today. Today, she felt like a person who'd been existing on caffeine—jittery and unable to concentrate.

Yes, she was avoiding Hayes. Avoiding her feelings. Avoiding the truth.

She didn't want to talk to him. She didn't want to give him the chance to let her down easy or tell her it had been a mistake, that they really needed to keep things the way they were. She didn't want to face the fact that he wasn't looking for a relationship, and they both knew she would never be a casual fling.

He was in Nantucket to take her to this party—and though she'd considered it, backing out would've been rude. Not speaking to him would've also been rude.

So here she was, standing in front of him, knowing exactly what she had to do.

She had to let him off the hook.

"I'm not avoiding you," she lied.

He wore a gray suit with a dusty blue and silver tie that somehow made his eyes look brighter. "I was kidding. I know you've been busy."

Right. Busy making excuses not to see him.

"We need to talk, Pru," he said. "About last night."

She shook her head and shrugged at the same time. "Don't even give it a second thought. I know it was nothing—just a mistake."

His smile faded. "A mistake."

"Yes," she said. "You said you screwed things up, but you didn't. I promise. I don't want things to be weird between us, and I know we make great friends, so we'll just pretend it never happened. It was stupid." Her laugh sounded ridiculous even to her.

Was he buying this? Because she certainly wasn't.

"Right," he said. "Of course." He flashed that smile, cool as ever, horribly unaware of what it did to her on the inside. "You got my texts, right? About Peggy?"

She nodded. "I did." She tried to play it cool too. Somehow, she thought perhaps she wasn't quite as successful.

Hayes had shared his plan with her via text the night before. Pru hadn't bothered to argue—but part of her wondered if maybe Pru and Hayes were foolish to think they could match two people with a past like Howie and Peggy's.

How many chances did people have to find true love?

No amount of magic could rewrite history, after all.

"You ready to go in?"

She nodded as he motioned toward the crowd. She took a step and felt his hand on the small of her back, leading her through the sea of people. She tensed at the contact.

Just friends.

"Are you okay?" he asked. "Nervous?"

"No," she said, aware that his body was *very* close to hers. Was he doing that on purpose? "I'm okay."

He led her through the room, stopping regularly to make small talk with the party's many attendees. Many people wanted to congratulate Pru for being chosen as the artist to design the talking tree. One couple stopped them to tell them to be sure to try the sliders. Two different people wanted to chat about surfing.

Pru did her best to stay upbeat and not to overthink the way Hayes stayed by her side, fetched her drinks, watched her talk. After forty-five minutes of mingling, he pulled her into a corner faintly lit by a Christmas tree that was part of the display, which did not seem like a *just friends* thing to do. The din of commotion died down as he moved her out of the high traffic area in favor of the quiet space where she could almost pretend they were alone. The chatter of conversation faded to nothing as he met her eyes and smiled.

He leaned in, close enough to make her heart flip-flop. Close enough that when he spoke, she felt his breath on her cheek. His hand was on the wall behind her, but she felt anything but trapped.

"I don't know if anyone's told you this yet," he said. "But you look incredible."

Just friends. She could tell herself that—tell him that—a million times in a single minute, but her heart was not getting the message.

She smoothed a hand over her emerald green party dress—the perfect balance of dressy/casual—and tried to ignore the quickening of her pulse. "Thanks," she whispered. "So do you."

Then, as if he was completely unfazed, he slid his hand around hers and led her back through the room. Onlookers might assume they were more than friends. The photographer who snapped their photo in front of the surfboard-themed replica of the talking tree she'd decorated might assume they were more than friends.

And if she didn't tell herself otherwise over and over again, she might also assume they were more than friends.

Because something in the air between them had changed, making her think that maybe kissing him hadn't been a mistake at all.

Howie arrived, wearing his "nice jeans," which apparently meant the ones without the holes in them, and a graphic T-shirt under a black blazer. Pru watched from her spot near the stairs as Peggy stared at him from across the room. He sauntered in, took one look at her, and Pru was sure she didn't imagine the connection between them.

Peggy might be hurt, and she might be playing hard to get, but she loved that man.

"Did you feel it?" Hayes asked.

Pru glanced at him, painting a question on her face.

"Magic." He whispered the word with a raise of his eyebrows, then smiled. "We're on."

"I'm not sure about this plan," Pru said, feeling suddenly nervous.

"We just need to get them alone together." He looked down at her. "A lot can happen when two people are alone."

Well, heck. She knew that was true.

She dared to meet his eyes. Bright and sparkling with promise, as always, and yet there was something different there too.

He didn't look away, as if he hadn't yet made his point.

"It didn't work very well last night," she said, thinking of how sad Peggy had seemed on their quiet walk home. She hadn't said hardly a word, but she didn't need to. Pru understood heartache. If Pru had to guess, she would say seeing Howie had stirred up all those old feelings in Peggy, and maybe she simply needed time to process them.

"It worked pretty good for us," he said.

Her breath caught. Was he . . . flirting with her? About the kiss, which she'd thought they'd agreed to never speak of again? And if he was, she should be angry, but mostly she was just trying to keep herself from going weak in the knees.

"I have a good feeling about this," Hayes said, as if his words had zero effect on her.

"Okay," she said. "I'll go get Howie."

He nodded, still looking at her, still unnerving her. She loved him, and she almost didn't care if he knew.

She took a step back. "See you in a minute." She walked away, aware that he was watching her.

Not so discreetly, she turned around and confirmed her suspicion. He lifted a hand in a wave, then walked away.

This charade had lost its appeal. At any moment, she feared she would bubble over with the truth. The words raced around in her mind like a dog chasing its tail.

I love you, Hayes. I've always loved you. I was just too scared of losing you to tell you the truth.

She shoved the words aside.

It was the Christmas magic working overtime. The gentle covering of snow blanketing the cobblestone outside. The beautifully decorated trees sparkling all over the room. The smells of delicious food, brought in from several local restaurants, filling the air.

And her overactive imagination.

That's all it was.

She found Howie chatting with a chef. When Pru walked up, she caught a snippet of their conversation about lobsters, which Howie seemed thoroughly engrossed in. When he noticed her, his grin widened.

"There's the woman of the hour," he said. "Love the tree, Pru. The whole vibe is spot-on. Is the big one covered in surfboards too?"

She smiled. "Thanks, Howie. And yes. I made tons of small surfboard ornaments. All hand painted. You don't think it's too bright?" She'd chosen to stick with summer colors for the replica tree, a perfect match of the twenty-foot tree on Main Street. She'd decorated each with hundreds of small pink, turquoise, orange, and green surfboards, each one a tiny work of art.

Nontraditional Christmas was just as fun as traditional Christmas, and Pru felt like her tree celebrated both.

"'Bout time we got some color around here," he said. "Seems like everything is white these days."

She smiled. "Hey, do you have a minute?"

"Sure thing." He gave the chef a nod and followed Pru off into the crowd. She knew the plan. She passed by the coat check where a young kid named Tad was working. As she walked by, he handed her a coat, then gave her a nod. He'd done his part to earn that handsome tip Hayes had slipped him earlier in one of their turns around the room.

"Where are we going?" Howie asked as she led him through the crowd and up the stairs.

"You'll see."

"You know that chef was about to give me the secret recipe for his lobster rolls, Pru," Howie said, trailing behind. "You interrupted what could've been a really important conversation."

She didn't bother to tell him the really important conversation was the one he'd have in a few minutes. Instead, she pressed on until she came to the door that led out to the rooftop. In the summer, it was a coveted wedding venue. In the winter, it was cold.

But it was also the only private spot in the museum she and Hayes could think of.

Howie chattered on as they made their way up the stairs. "Aren't they going to introduce you as the artist of the year or something? Seems like maybe you should stick close to the action."

"Not artist of the year," she said. "Just designer of the talking tree."

"But this is like, your coming out party. Didn't you always want to be a society girl?"

She laughed. "Do you know me at all?"

She pushed the door at the top of the stairway open, and a chill hit her lungs. Howie might not appreciate what was about to happen, but she hoped it would be worth it. They walked closer to the edge of the rooftop, and Pru handed Howie the coat. "Would you hold this for me?"

"Sure, but what are we doing out here?"

"Enjoying the view," she said. "I mean, you were the one who taught me if I didn't like something in my life, maybe I just needed to change my view."

He pushed a hand through his longish salt-and-pepper hair, then pulled his suitcoat tighter. "So, you don't like something about your life?"

She heard voices behind them. They turned and found Peggy and Hayes standing in the doorway. Peggy stopped at the sight of Howie, and Hayes seemed to be pushing her forward.

"Did you guys need some air too?" Hayes asked.

Howie hadn't stopped looking at Peggy since she appeared.

"Hey, Peg," he said. "Did you get the flowers?"

Peggy glanced at Hayes, then back at Howie. It looked like she might bolt right off the roof and back to the party at any moment.

"Yes," she said quietly. "Thank you."

Well, that was a start. At least she wasn't heading for the door.

"Didn't know anyone would be out here," Hayes said. "Peggy was showing me the roof because I have an event this summer that I thought might be perfect up here."

"Is that right?" Howie asked, not buying it for a second. Peggy, on the other hand, seemed oblivious.

"You're right, Peggy," Hayes said. "It's got a killer view." He glanced at Pru. "How many does it seat?"

Peggy stuttered for a brief second, then seemed to gather herself, launching into what sounded like a well-rehearsed sales pitch. Peggy knew everything about this building the same way she knew everything about every other historical building on the island. Her love of Nantucket was well-documented. She took a few steps off to the side, chattering about the seating and the view and the best time of day for a summer party.

Pru glanced at Howie, who seemed enamored with this plain schoolteacher. The way he looked at her—like she was the only person in the world—well, it could turn even her into a romantic.

At some point during her speech, he must've realized he was holding Peggy's coat, because he took a step forward and helped her put it on.

Peggy stopped talking and looked out over the dimly lit island, a hush coming over them.

"You're still wearing it," Howie said.

Peggy looked caught, her eyes wide, as she glanced at Howie. Her hand followed his eyes to the necklace dangling at her neck. She quietly tucked it under her coat.

Howie took a step toward her, then reached over and

pulled the necklace out so it was visible again. "It looks nice on you."

It was dark outside, but Pru could still see the blush on Peggy's cheeks. The older woman cleared her throat.

"I didn't mean for you to see that," Peggy said.

Hayes took a step toward Pru, but neither of them spoke. The movement must've reminded Howie they weren't alone.

"I gave her that necklace when we were kids," Howie said. "For graduation."

"You went to school together," Hayes said, as if piecing together a puzzle.

Howie stayed focused on Peggy. "We did. And when we graduated, Peggy was the one who planned to travel the world. She was quite the adventurer."

Pru frowned. That didn't sound like Peggy. As far as Pru knew, the older woman had never been off the island. What had changed?

"What is the necklace?" Pru asked.

"It's a compass," Peggy said. "On the back, it says 'For my true north.'" She picked up the necklace and turned it over between her fingers.

Howie's smile faded. "You were, too. You kept me in line."

Peggy's cheeks turned pink.

"You still up for an adventure, Peg? With me?"

They stared at each other for a long moment, so long that Pru started to feel like an intruder. Finally, Peggy looked away.

"I'm not sure this is a good time to have this conversation," she said.

"We'll give you two some privacy." Hayes gave Pru's

arm a tug. When she looked at him, he motioned with his head for her to follow him. As they slowly crept toward the door, Howie took a step toward Peggy.

"Peggy, there are a few things I need to say."

Before they heard anymore, Pru and Hayes slipped off the roof and into the stairwell.

Pru glanced at Hayes. "We're just going to leave them out there?"

He started down the stairs. "Yep."

"On the rooftop in December?"

"Yep." He grinned. "They're adults. They'll be fine."

"They're gonna freeze," Pru said.

Hayes waggled his eyebrows. "Maybe they'll think of a creative way to stay warm."

She rolled her eyes. "What do you think—they're going to have one conversation and suddenly everything will be okay?"

He went completely still and his gaze dipped from her eyes to her lips and back again. "Is that so hard to imagine? A lot could be worked out if they'd just be honest with each other."

Pru's heart thudded in her chest, like the sound of a bass drum in a marching band. Her thoughts turned to that kiss. A kiss that almost set her on fire. A kiss she should absolutely regret but didn't. A kiss that had only left her longing for more.

Hayes was right—she'd tried to deny it, but it was high time for honesty.

He was close to her now, at the bottom of the stairwell, hidden away from the rest of the world.

She took a step back, losing her resolve, forgetting why it was they couldn't be together. And he was looking at her *like that*, and she wanted to pretend they weren't Pru and Hayes. She wanted to pretend it was perfectly okay for them to make out right there in the middle of a Christmas party in which she was a guest of honor.

"I should go." She took a step back and ran into a door.

He didn't look away, but he nodded slowly. "You should. Because if you don't, I'm going to kiss you again."

She cleared her throat but didn't move. Was this *magic* he talked about working overtime? Had they been smacked with some sort of crazy Christmas spell or were they simply two lonely people who knew each other too well?

"Hayes, I'm scared," she whispered.

"I know," he said. "And I am too. But you and I—we make sense."

"Do we?"

He took her hands in his. "Peggy told me the best relationships start out as friends," He paused, searching her eyes. "Do you know you're the only person who knows about Egypt?"

"Not even your parents?" Pru asked quietly. "Or Hollis?"

He shook his head. "Just you. And the only time I stop thinking about what I saw is when I'm with you."

She didn't have a reason to argue. She'd been carrying a torch for him for how many years? What was she so afraid of now that everything she'd wanted was right in front of her.

"I don't want to be like Howie and Peggy, Prudence. I don't want you to be the one that got away."

Inexplicably, tears sprang to her eyes.

"But you're . . ." she searched for the words.

"I'm?"

"You're you."

He half-laughed. "Last time I checked, that was true."

"Maybe you're just confused."

"Why is it so hard for you believe that I'm in love with you?"

Her heart stopped.

"And why is it so hard for you to admit you love me too?"

She lifted her chin to level his gaze and found nothing but authenticity waiting for her there.

"You have this whole big, wonderful family, and I have you," she said. "I can't risk that. I can't screw that up."

"You aren't," he said, pushing her hair away from her face. "You're just making it better."

"Hayes—"

He studied her—too intently, in fact, and it sent her insides tumbling.

He inched closer. "Tell me you don't feel it."

She swallowed. Her throat was dry. This was the part where she either told him she felt nothing for him and raced off or she gave in to every human desire that coursed through her body.

"Pru." Her name was husky on his lips, a faint whisper, the stuff dreams are made of.

"Prudence Sutton!" A man's voice rang out from somewhere in the main room, where the party was still underway.

"Oh no!" She gasped. "They're introducing me right now. This is going to look so bad. You stay here while I run out there so it doesn't look like—you know. . ."

"Like what?" He grinned.

"Hayes." Heat rushed to her cheeks.

"Not a chance," Hayes said. "I came here to watch you go up on that stage and talk about your tree. No way I'm missing it."

"Prudence Sutton!?" This time, there was a question in the announcer's voice.

She pulled the door open just as Hayes grabbed her free hand, spinning her back to face him. He kissed her so fully and in plain view of at least half of the party-goers, clearly not minding one little bit that they'd just been caught in a very awkward-looking situation.

But once he released her and sent her back into the main area, she couldn't help but notice her knees had gone weak and the only thing she could think about was getting through this speech so they could finish their conversation.

CHAPTER 16

FADED PHOTOGRAPHS

*H*ayes watched Pru take the stage. Her cheeks were red with embarrassment, and he felt mildly bad for his part in that, but mostly he just wanted her to hurry up so they could ditch the party and be alone.

"Thank you so much," Pru said. "And thank you to my friends and adopted family who came to the island to be here for this event tonight. I'm so honored to have had the chance to take my love of making custom surfboards and tie it in with my love of Christmas. The talking tree has been one of my favorite Stroll events since I first came to the island right after high school, so this is truly a full circle moment for me."

Hayes wasn't even going to pretend he was unaffected by her beauty, her kindness, the way she knew him so well. He'd been living in complete denial, but now that he realized it, he was sure of only one thing—he didn't want to spend another moment without Pru.

And not just as a friend.

Behind him, the door to the stairway that led to the roof opened, and Peggy rushed out.

"Peggy," he called out after her, but the woman kept on walking, straight out the front door.

Howie appeared in the doorway, a sheepish look on his face. He glanced at Hayes, then walked off toward the bar.

"That was some entrance you two made." Hollis stood at Hayes's side.

Hayes tossed a glance at his brother, and smirked.

"'Bout time," Harper said, coming up on his other side.

"What's that supposed to mean?" Hayes returned his gaze to the small stage where the head of the Nantucket Chamber was questioning Pru about her artwork.

"Please," Harper said. "We've all been waiting for this for like, ten years."

"It's good to see you finally figured it out," Hollis said.

The crowd applauded and Pru exited the stage, smiling as she zig-zagged her way through the room. She stopped to chat with Hayes's parents, then made her way over to him.

"Did you see that Peggy left?" she asked, meeting Hayes's eyes.

He nodded. "Yeah."

"I think I'm going to go make sure she's okay," she said.

"No," he said. "I'll go. "You need to stay here—it's your party."

"Okay," she said. "I'll catch up with you later?"

He wanted to kiss her. He wanted to lead her back to the stairwell and finish what they'd almost started. Instead, he nodded and walked off. It wasn't lost on him

him that Pru hadn't given him any indication of how she felt about him.

She was hesitant, that was clear. How could he convince her to take a chance on him? How could he show her they were perfect for each other?

Before he grabbed his coat to leave and check on Peggy, Hayes wandered over to the bar, where Howie sat, a nearly empty glass in front of him.

Hayes sat down next to him. "What happened up there?"

Howie shrugged. "It was going so well. Kind of like old times. We have a lot of catching up to do, and for the first time, I thought maybe we had a shot. Maybe she still had feelings for me."

"And?"

"And it was great until I told her I'm not staying for the Christmas Stroll. I came to town for Pru, and I leave Saturday."

Hayes frowned. "Can't you change your plans?"

"That's what Peggy asked." Howie frowned. "Then the conversation turned. Said something about setting herself up for disappointment and not getting hurt again. Then she raced off. I guess she got spooked."

Hayes thought back to the moment she emerged from the stairwell. She certainly did look spooked.

The bartender pushed a glass toward Howie, who picked it up and drained it with a sigh.

"I never thought I'd get another chance with Peggy. It wasn't even on my radar. She's been pretty cold to me over the years, so I just assumed it wasn't in the cards."

"And now?"

"Now, I'd do just about anything to win her over,"

Howie said. "Even move back here in the middle of December, although I think we'd have a much better time if she retired and we traveled while we're still young enough to enjoy it."

Howie pulled his wallet out of his back pocket. He opened it and pulled out a small photograph, folded in half. He handed it to Hayes. "I've been carrying that around since I moved off the island."

"What is it?" Hayes looked down at the image and a young woman with bright eyes stared back at him. He unfolded it and saw a younger, shirtless Howie with the same shoulder-length hair he had now standing at the woman's side. "Is that you and Peggy?"

Howie looked away. "Found it when I moved. It was in a box of old things Tammy had shoved in the attic."

"You know what I think?" Hayes asked.

Howie's eyes seem to welcome any suggestions.

"I think you need to show her you're serious. Don't leave Saturday. Change your plans. Isn't she worth it?"

The bartender returned with another cocktail for the older man. Howie picked it up, looked at Hayes, and shook his head. "I messed it all up, kid. A long time ago. And that woman"—he pointed to the photo—"if she was ever in love with that guy—she's not anymore."

Hayes watched as Howie strolled off. He glanced down and saw that Howie had left the old photo on the counter. He picked it up and looked at it. Peggy was looking straight at the camera, but Howie was looking straight at Peggy, and the admiration on his face was undeniable.

He reached into his back pocket and tugged out his own wallet, opened it, and pulled out his own folded, but not quite as faded, photograph. He and Pru on the beach the second summer after they'd met. Hayes had his arm draped around Pru's shoulder, and she was grinning at the camera. But Hayes was smiling at her.

Maybe it was time he took his own advice.

HAYES LEFT THE PARTY, Howie's photo in his pocket, drove toward the edge of town and stopped in front of a small gray-shingled cottage. A lone light shone in the living room, and while he knew it was risky to show up this late, he had to try.

And he also knew that time mattered. After all, anyone, including Howie, could leave the island at any moment.

He knocked on the front door and waited until Peggy opened it. She still wore her party outfit, but there were fluffy slippers on her feet.

"Hayes."

He smiled what he was certain was a sad smile, a mirror image of her own. "Sorry to show up unan-nounced."

"Oh, I don't mind." Peggy's smile looked forced. "Do you want to come in?"

"That's okay. I just wanted to see if you were okay."

A quizzical expression washed over her face. "Oh. Yes, I'm okay."

"And I wanted to give you this." Hayes pulled the photo out of his pocket and handed it to her.

Peggy took the old picture, and her eyes turned glassy. One hand covered her slight gasp. "Where did you get this?"

"Peggy, I don't know what happened between you and Howie all those years ago or tonight on the roof, but I do know one thing for sure."

She looked up at him, eyes expectant, as if Hayes had the magic words that could take her pain away. And maybe he did.

"He loves you."

Peggy's face softened. "You can't possibly know that."

"I can," he said. "And I do. He's not doing a very good job of hiding how he really feels about you."

"There's a lot you don't know, Mr. McGuire."

Hayes pulled his coat tighter around his body. "I know. And maybe it won't be simple." He paused. "I just know if you gave him another chance, you'd make him the happiest man alive."

Peggy pushed the photo toward Hayes.

His hands went up, as if to reject her offering. "You keep it. Maybe it'll remind you that once upon a time, you two had something special. Magical even. And that doesn't come along every day."

She pulled her hand back and studied the image again. "Thank you, Hayes."

"Now, the other reason I came. . ." He put on his best version of a charming smile and hoped for the best. Because if anyone could help him make this idea a reality, it was Peggy, one of the most well-connected people in Nantucket.

CHAPTER 17

A SURPRISE STOP

*P*ru had watched Hayes talk to Howie, and then walk out the front door of the Nantucket Whaling Museum, and for a brief moment, she considered running after him and spilling the truth about how she felt.

But no, it could wait for a time when they weren't rushed or surrounded by people.

She'd finished out the evening with a throat sore from all the talking she'd done. Once she was back home in her most comfortable pair of pajamas, she replayed the unfinished conversation she and Hayes had had in the stairwell. She closed her eyes and thought about the kiss he'd stolen as she left him standing there, the way it had sent a tingle straight down her spine, the way she still felt it now, hours later.

The following morning, Pru dragged herself out of bed and checked her phone. Nothing from Hayes.

She showered, dressed and made herself some coffee, then checked her phone again. Still nothing.

Around 10:00 a.m., there was a knock at the door, and her heart leapt and relaxed at the same time. *Finally!* She raced over and pulled it open, but it wasn't Hayes standing on the doorstep. It was his mom and sister.

And they both wore smiles so big they had to be fake.

"What's wrong?" Pru asked.

Nan frowned, then looked at Harper. "Do we look like something's wrong?"

Harper shrugged. "I thought we looked full of Christmas cheer."

Pru frowned. "You're not here to tell me Hayes left on the early morning ferry or something, are you?"

They both stared at her.

"Sorry, come in." She pulled the door open, and they passed by. "I'm just hoping to talk to him is all."

"About that kiss?" Harper's eyebrows bounced.

Pru looked at her, then at Nan, whose smile seemed to suggest that yes, she'd seen it too.

"Just about stuff," Pru said.

"Well, we're here to take you out. We haven't been in Nantucket for the Christmas Stroll in ages, so we want to take full advantage." Nan held up a small booklet that Pru recognized immediately as the program for the Christmas Stroll. There was a profile of her and the surf shop inside, along with a list of every event that was happening that weekend. She flipped it open. "I made an itinerary, and I was sure to hit all the best spots."

"Oh, really?" Pru tried to muster some enthusiasm, but truthfully, she just wanted to go find Hayes.

"There's an ugly sweater contest and then lunch at the Nantucket Hotel," Nan said, flipping through the booklet. "Of course, we can stop in any of the boutiques in town, and I found a modern calligraphy class—I've always wanted to try that. Then I thought we could do the Holiday House tour to close out the day."

"That's a lot," Pru said.

"Like I said, I want to take full advantage." Nan's smile matched Harper's. How could Pru say no?

"Do you know what Hayes is doing today?" Pru asked.

"Oh, he and his dad left early this morning," Nan said. "Who knows what they're doing? Are you ready? Is there anything on this list you want to skip?"

"Maybe the ugly sweaters?" Pru grimaced.

"Oh, thank goodness," Harper said. She reached into her bag and pulled out a hideous Christmas green sweater with strands of actual tinsel and gold and red glass ornaments attached to it. "I really did not want to wear this."

Pru laughed. "Are you sure? I think you might actually win with that."

Harper tossed it in the garbage and turned toward the door. "Let's go."

On the way to the Nantucket Hotel, they stopped to watch as Pru's decorated Christmas tree "talked" to the children who dared to stop in front of it.

"Is there a video camera in there?" Nan asked, squinting.

"I'll never tell," Pru said, though in truth, she didn't know. All she knew is that someone from the Nantucket Chamber was seated in the window of City Hall, right behind the tree. He spoke to the kids by way of a microphone, and judging by their reactions, the event was a hit.

Nan linked arms with Pru. "You should be very proud."

She tried to swat the compliment away, as usual, but somehow, this one penetrated her heart.

They walked on toward the hotel, where they found a spot on the glass enclosed terrace. They ordered from the ala carte menu and Pru checked her phone a thousand times, wondering why Hayes had gone radio silent.

Was he having second thoughts? Wishing he could take back what he said the night before? Regretting the way their relationship had changed?

She shoved the thoughts aside and forced herself to be rational.

After they ate, they stopped at a craft show where Harper picked up a turtle ornament and Nan bought a wreath made entirely of seashells. They stopped in three different boutiques and Mitchell's Book Corner and Pru browsed, but mostly continued to check her phone.

"Dear," Nan said as they settled into their seats for the modern calligraphy class. "You seem preoccupied."

"I'm sorry. I am a little distracted," Pru said. "Hayes didn't say anything when he got home last night, did he?"

"Anything like what, dear?"

Like he loves me? "Oh, I don't know. We didn't really get to say goodbye last night. I guess I just wondered . . ."

At her pause, Nan finished the sentence. "Where things stood?"

Pru nodded.

"Well, there is only one way to find out," Nan said. "When you see him again, you can ask him."

Pru glanced down at the supplies on the table in front of her. "What if this is all a big mistake?"

Nan picked up her pen and started writing her name. "Well, then, you learn from it."

"But I don't want to lose him, Nan," Pru said.

She stopped writing and looked at Pru. "It's a risk.

Love is messy. But life is messy too, and the regret of not trying could far outweigh the regret of everything falling apart."

The teacher, a young woman wearing a Santa hat and a valid contender for the ugly sweater contest, took her place at the front of the classroom and began teaching. Pru half-listened to the instruction, turning Nan's words over in her mind. It was the last boost she needed to bolster her bravery.

Whenever she finally saw Hayes, she would tell him exactly how she felt, and she wouldn't overthink it. She'd just be honest.

Though, as the minutes ticked by, it began to seem more and more like she wasn't going to see him at all today.

The class ended (Pru was *not* a modern calligrapher) and the three of them headed in the direction of the Holiday Home Tour. She was getting tired, and frankly, a little impatient. Where was Hayes?

She finally texted him: *Everything okay?*

But there was no reply.

The three historic homes on the Holiday House Tour were, as expected, remarkable. They'd each been professionally decorated for Christmas, and there were guides from the Nantucket Historical society to explain what was known about the history of each house. Pru's modest cottage felt like a dollhouse compared to these homes, and yet, she was certain she preferred it over these. It may not have an interesting history, or a lot of square footage, but it was hers.

Nan stopped on the sidewalk outside the last house on the tour and let out a small, contented sigh. "I'm so glad we came here for the holidays, Prudence. This day and being with you girls has reminded me what the season is really about."

"I'm glad you made it," Pru said. "It means a lot to me to have you here." She glanced at Harper. "All of you. Thanks for spending the day with me, too."

"Oh, we aren't quite done," Nan said.

Pru tried to shake her disappointment. She thought for sure she was going to be able to go home and call Hayes. As the day had worn on, she'd grown increasingly more worried that he had, in fact, left the island, that his mom and sister felt so badly about his rash decision to take off they were trying to distract her, to postpone her heartache.

Ridiculous? Maybe. But at the moment, it seemed likely.

"I thought we did everything on the itinerary," Pru said. "No?"

They walked down the block and turned the corner, then started down another street, this one lined with much smaller, neatly decorated cottages than the homes they'd just visited. They stopped in front of a gray shingled cottage with white trim and a dusty blue door.

"Here we are," Nan said. "A surprise stop."

Harper appeared to be holding in a squeal.

Pru frowned. "A surprise?" She didn't much care for surprises. "A surprise for who?"

But Nan was already walking toward the door, Harper close on her heels. Pru had no choice but to follow. Would they have thought her rude if she gently explained she didn't really have much Christmas spirit at the moment, that she really only wanted to find Hayes, profess her love and live happily ever after? Or take her rejection in private?

They stood on the porch now. "Who lives here?"

Pru's question went ignored. Seconds later, the door opened and Peggy Swinton stood on the other side.

This wasn't Peggy's house. She'd walked her home only days ago, and it was on the other end of town.

"Good afternoon," Peggy said. "Come in."

"Peggy, what are you doing here?" Pru asked, coming in out of the cold.

Peggy smiled. "I'm your official tour guide." She launched into a history of the little home, which, apparently had been in her family for a number of years. "In recent years, we've secured long-term renters, but we've never been tempted to sell. She may not be as grand as the homes you've just toured, but she is not without her charm."

Peggy spoke exactly as she would have if she were leading the tour through one of Nantucket's oldest and most beautiful homes. Pru tried to pay attention, not wanting to be rude, but she couldn't help but check her phone.

Where was Hayes? Why hadn't he called or at least texted her? Things were so uncertain between them, and dragging this out was agony.

"Perhaps my favorite feature of this house," Peggy said now, "is the back yard. It's got a stunning view of Brant Point Lighthouse, and tomorrow, if you've got a pair of binoculars, you'll even catch a glimpse of the Coast Guard cutter bringing Santa into town." She opened the door and motioned for Pru to walk through to outside, but when she did, the door closed behind her and she found herself standing on the deck—alone.

By now, the daylight had begun to fade, and when she looked up, she realized there were swaths of greenery and white lights strung through a pergola overhead.

She turned around just as Hayes came around the back of the house and stopped in front of her, several feet away.

What was he doing here?

He stood still for a long moment, watching her, the two of them doing nothing but breathing, and it took every bit of her willpower not to run straight to him and let out the string of emotions she'd kept bottled up for so many years.

"Pru." Her name left his lips in a hush.

Confusion turned a circle in her head, but she said nothing.

The weight of his gaze pressed down on her, and the words she'd been replaying in her mind over and over had vanished. She couldn't think of a single thing to say.

He walked toward her, bathed in the warm glow of the white lights above.

"Hi," he said.

She smiled. "Hi."

"Did you have a good day?" Something sparked in his eyes.

"Did you set that up?" she asked.

He shrugged. "Maybe. I had some things to work out."

"I did have a good day," she said. "But mostly I've been wanting to find you."

"Is that right?"

She looked away, losing her nerve.

He took a step toward her. "Do you want to dance?"

"There's no music."

He pulled out his phone, tapped around on it and landed on Michael Bublé's rendition of "Have Yourself a Merry Little Christmas." The orchestra swelled, and then the deep, rich tone of his voice. She'd always loved this song.

She'd always loved this man.

He opened his arms to her. "Shall we?"

She waited a beat, then stepped closer, not noticing at all the way his hand felt on the small of her back or how he pressed her body ever-so-slightly toward his own. And definitely not paying attention to his delicious, masculine scent or the way his cheek was practically pressed to hers. He took her hand and held it to his chest as they swayed to the music, and Pru was certain she'd just gotten lost in the most perfect moment of her life.

He spun her around, and behind them, she could see several pairs of eyes watching from inside. Both of Hayes's parents, Harper, Peggy and—Pru stiffened. "Is that Howie?"

Hayes followed her gaze inside, where the nosy onlookers finally got the hint and moved away from the window.

"Are they holding hands?" Pru stopped moving.

Hayes grinned. "I think they worked it out."

"Really?" Pru was surprised how happy that made her. Sure, she was rooting for them, but also, seeing Howie and Peggy together made her feel like anything was possible—even best friends falling in love.

"What do you think changed?" Pru asked.

"I think Howie finally figured out how to show Peggy he was serious about her," Hayes said.

"Oh?"

"Yeah, he's going to stick around for a few months," Hayes said.

They began to sway again, and she relished the way it felt to be in his arms.

"And so am I."

The words hung between them, but she didn't dare move for fear of realizing she'd misunderstood.

"Did you hear me, Pru?"

The music swelled, and Hayes held her tighter, looking out past her as they danced. His face was next to hers, his arms firmly around her, and they moved like that for long moments, their breathing synchronized in the movement of the dance.

She nodded.

"I brought you here because I wanted to show you my new place. I signed a year lease on this house," Hayes said. "I wanted to show you I'm ready. I'll work my whole life to become the man you deserve."

"But why? Why not just stay at your parents' house?"

"That's not a commitment," Hayes said. "If I was living there, I could walk away anytime. Here, I'm contractually obligated. And I want you to know I'm not going anywhere. I'm done pretending."

"Pretending about . . . ?"

"Me and you," he said, still not looking at her. "I pretended the day I told you we could just be friends, and I've been pretending ever since." He stopped moving and looked at her. "I don't want to be your friend, Pru. And maybe I've always known that or maybe I just realized it this week—I don't know. But now that I know it, there's no way I can keep pretending. There's no way I can go back to my life unless you're in it."

Her eyes clouded and she looked at him, beautiful and earnest and everything she ever wanted. They fit, she and Hayes, better than she ever could've imagined.

"I don't know how you feel about me," he said. "But I know one thing. I know I love you. And not just like a friend. I'm in love with you, Pru. I think I always have been. I think that's why I've never really been serious with anyone else. Because none of the other girls were you."

A tear slid down her cheek. "Do you know how long I've waited to hear you say that?"

He wiped the tear away with his thumb. "So, what you're saying is, we should've done this a long time ago?"

She laughed. "Maybe we should've."

"Why didn't we?" he asked. "Why didn't you say something?"

"I was scared."

"Of what?"

"Losing you."

"Not possible," Hayes said. "You're stuck with me now. If that's okay with you, I mean."

"It's more than okay." She reached over and touched his face, the stubble on his chin slightly rough under her fingers.

They looked at each other for a beat, and then he grinned. "Did you hear the part where I said I love you?"

"I did hear that." She couldn't help it, she grinned right back. "And in case you're wondering, I love you too."

"Yeah?"

She nodded. "And not like a friend."

His arms circled her waist and he pulled her body close to his. A breeze skittered over the backyard, and Michael Bublé crooned "The Christmas Song" from the phone in Hayes's pocket. He ran a thumb over her bottom lip, then covered her mouth with his, kissing her slowly, deeply, purposefully, like a man intent on cherishing every last bit of her.

"We're just going to go, Hayes," Peggy called out from inside the house. "Howie and I have a date."

He pulled away from Pru and smiled knowingly. "Bye everyone," he called out, not taking his eyes off of Pru.

"Noni Rose strikes again," she said without looking away.

"What can I say, I've got the touch." He tucked a stray hair behind her ear. "Now do you believe in magic?"

"Now do you believe in soulmates?"

"I believe in us." He leaned down and kissed her, with all the kindness of a friend she knew she would love for the rest of her life.

EPILOGUE

*N*ellie returned from Paris a week after Christmas to find the Noni Rose box on her porch, a crisp envelope taped inside.

She smiled as she walked up the stairs to her office, eager to catch up on her matchmaking duties but also eager to finally, finally, put to rest one of the most difficult matches she'd taken on in her entire matchmaking career.

Prudence Sutton wasn't only stubborn, she was in love, and from the moment Nellie realized it, she knew she wouldn't rest until the dark-headed beauty was finally happy. And that meant doing a bit of pushing, which, anyone who knew her would tell you, she was quite happy to do.

Nellie opened the crisp white envelope to find a photo of Pru and her darling favorite nephew. She flipped it over to reveal, in Hayes's handwriting: *Our first Christmas together.*

"Did it work?" Arthur stood in the doorway of the office, a wry smile on his face.

"Like a charm." Nellie smiled as she fixed the photo neatly into the well-worn book of Noni Rose success stories right next to the wedding announcement of Howie Basford and Peggy Swinton.

Like a charm.

THE END

A NOTE FROM THE AUTHOR

Dear Reader,

If you know me or follow me on social media, you know how much I love Christmas stories. Every Christmas themed movie is going in my queue, and I am going to deck myself out in holiday garb to watch with utter glee.

Usually, I'll even share my reviews on Instagram as I watch.

How was it possible, then, that I've only ever written ONE book set at Christmas? I knew that had to change. And, even better, I knew I needed a writing project that was purely for fun.

Naturally, I thought of Nantucket, where a few of my other books are set. It's an island full of charm, and I knew that charm hung around long after the summer season ended. The Christmas traditions on Nantucket are a small-town romance author's dream, so it was absolute joy to immerse myself in that world as I revisited a beloved member of my cast, Hayes McGuire.

Charming, adorable, younger brother Hayes was one of my favorite characters to write in *If For Any Reason*, so I knew he needed a very special heroine. And I was so very happy when Pru burst onto the page.

Thank you so much for spending a bit of the holiday season with Pru and Hayes (and, I suppose, with me.) You can't possibly understand what a gift it is for me to know that you've made time for one of my stories. I hope you enjoyed it. I hope it swept you away for a while, and that it instantly put you in the Christmas spirit.

As always, I LOVE to connect with my readers, so I invite you to find and follow me through my newsletter, on social media or in my Facebook Reader Room. I would absolutely love to see you there!

Drop me a line anytime—I love making new friends.

Courtney Walsh

Courtney Walsh is the Carol award-winning author of
*Just Look Up, Just Let Go, Just One Kiss, Just Like Home, If For
Any Reason, Things Left Unsaid, Hometown Girl, Paper
Hearts, Change of Heart,* and the Sweethaven series. Her
debut novel, *A Sweethaven Summer,* was a *New York Times*
and *USA Today* e-book best-seller and a Carol Award
finalist in the debut author category. In addition, she has
written two craft books and several full-length musicals.
Courtney lives with her husband and three children in
Illinois, where she co-owns a performing arts studio and
youth theatre with the best business partner she could
imagine—her husband.

Visit her online at www.courtneywalshwrites.com

Printed in Great Britain
by Amazon

32636889R00099